FAIRY DIRT

Prophecy of a Fae
Book One

BONNIE THOMLEY

FICTION WRITER
Bonnie Thomley

To my husband, thank you for supporting my dreams. You have given me a wonderful life and family, and nothing I accomplish will ever top that. I love you.

And behold the young fairy
with wings of the heavens
that will rise up
and save the realm of the mystica.

ONE

The morning fog was unusually thin as Brynn made her way to school. Normally at this time of day, you could barely see anything just a few paces in front of you. She walked alone, as was her normal morning routine. She could see the other fairies walking together about thirty feet ahead of her in the distance. They were chatting and laughing as if they didn't have a care in the world.

"Did you hear that Ashteline is dating one of the elder's sons?"

"What? Which one? Please not Braeden. He is way out of her league."

"She wishes! No, it's one of the lesser ones. Josh, I think. But anyways. He's been buying her all kinds of things and word on the street is that she is about to get a sweet new car."

"Must be nice to enjoy some of that elder power."

Shallow bitches. It was fine with her that they excluded her from their clique. She had been different her entire life and she had finally come to terms with that. They weren't the type of people that made good friends anyway. There was no real loyalty.

Brynn wasn't as pretty as the other girls. She definitely wasn't what you would expect a fairy to look like. Fairies, by general rule, were blonde with green eyes, bouncy and very shimmery. Their platinum hair usually had a rainbow undertone to it when the light caught it just right. It was beautiful. Humans go to hair salons and pay hundreds of dollars for that look. Fairies had it naturally. But not Brynn. She had light brown hair with ombre blue tips, blue eyes and there was certainly no shimmer to her. Even her wings were different. Normal fairy wings were silky and butterfly like. Hers were fluffy, feathery, and white... identical to angel wings. She felt like such a freak. She just sighed at the thought of being an outcast and focused on her walk to school.

The summers in the south were hot but they were beautiful. The scent of honeysuckles perfumed her walk to school. It was a smell that she could never get tired of. She inhaled deeply, letting the floral arrangement linger in her nose, savoring the moment as she saw her school up ahead.

She was thankful that she went to a normal high school with human kids. It was easy for her to blend in with them. She looked like all of the humans. They could tell that something was different with the other fairies, but Brynn just looked like an ordinary teenager. In that way, she didn't mind how she looked. That was the only case, though.

"We're going to the beach tonight, are you in?" Max asked as Brynn joined her group of friends standing on the sidewalk in front of the school. She took a quick glance around. The other fairies had already disappeared from sight. She let the thought of them fade away as she focused all of her attention on Max. That wasn't hard to do.

Max moved to town in the middle of the school year from Maddigan, which was several towns away. Brynn thought that he was absolutely beautiful. His thick dark hair set off his hazel, almost golden eyes. He was tall and very well built. He looked older than a lot of the other boys at her school. She loved the way his t-shirts clung tightly to his biceps, which were bigger than most of the guys there as well. It was amazing to her that a boy who looked the way that he did was so down to earth. His sculpted, jock appearance would ordinarily suggest otherwise. He was laid back and easy to carry on a conversation with. It was refreshing. Even if she wasn't crushing hard, she would still enjoy spending time with him.

"I can't go anywhere after school. I have to study tonight." Brynn said with a sincere frown. Max assumed that she meant either studying scripture or bible stories. This was an excuse that he had gotten used to getting from her. She relied on a religious façade to hide the truth about what she was. If someone found out that fairies were real and they actually *did* believe any of it, there would be serious consequences. It was instilled in them from the day they were born that one of the reasons their race had survived for so long was because of the stringent secrecy.

It was also because of that secrecy that Brynn couldn't be involved in any type of after school club or extracurricular activity. No girl scouts, no softball, just school. Most of the teenaged fairies wondered why they were even forced to go to a human school if they weren't supposed to get too close to people. They were told by the elders that it was a necessary step to learn to blend in with the human race. Public school was the best way to learn how to do that. She was allowed to have a few friends, though, and she spent as much time with them as possible. That went double for Max.

"I was afraid that would be your answer. I thought your family usually considered letting you out of the house on Friday nights. What's with the sudden change?" Max's sad puppy dog eyes would have made most girls cave and break the rules. He was disappointed at her response, but something about it made him feel a bit skeptical. It always felt like she was holding something back, but he couldn't put his finger on it. His expression gave his skepticism away, so Brynn knew she needed to pony up more information to sell her bullshit story.

"I have been slacking off all week and my mom isn't very happy about it. I guess this is part of my punishment. She knows it will torture me. Seriously, it's worse than water boarding."

He was right, there had been occasions here and there where she could be out after school on Fridays. It was usually for a school function. Even then she had to have documentation of the event to show her mom, and someone had to go with her. Like a chaperone. They were always obvious about it too. It was embarrassing, and a total pain in the butt. Totally not worth the trouble.

"Ok then, but it won't be as fun without you." Max leaned in a bit closer. "You were really the only one I wanted to hang out with." He whispered low enough that no one else could hear it. His soft breath on her neck made her shiver a bit. Despite the shiver, every other part of her turned red hot. She hoped he didn't notice.

She really wished that she could go to the beach. The salt air, Max shirtless in the water... ugh. It was what her daydreams were made of. She just smiled and shrugged her shoulders at him. The warning bell rang, and they headed into the school. Brynn walked as closely to Max as she could. She hated having to hide her feelings for him, but she had no choice. Telling him that he made her feel like a volcano erupting in the middle of a snowstorm would surely land her in a significant amount of trouble. She wished that she could just be truthful with him, though. How could she ever hope to keep a friendship with him if there wasn't trust?

She tried to avoid further conversation on the matter for the rest of the day. The more it was discussed, the more he could have a chance to get suspicious. Quickly coming up with answers to his questions wasn't her forte. He was extremely quick-witted. She envied that about him. He had a comeback for everything. Trying to get anything past him was going to be challenging. So, they simply enjoyed each other's company in the classes that they shared until it was time to go home.

She hadn't told Max a complete lie. She *did* have to study something. After school, it was time to practice magic and she really had been avoiding it throughout most of the week. It might as well have been the plague or something. Who could blame her? She was terrible at casting spells. It was humiliating. She had spent most of her time in her room listening to music and reading instead this week.

She loved her bedroom. It was her escape. Her queen-sized bed rested underneath a white canopy that hung from a mahogany four post bed frame. The oversized light blue silk comforter perfectly matched the curtains on the opposite side of the room. There were shelves full of books and cds that she listened to over and over. It was pretty outdated, but using the internet was not really allowed. Not having entertainment apps to use left no choice but to listen to music the old-fashioned way. She was lucky to even have a cell phone... even if it was just a primitive flip phone with a crappy camera. Either way, her room was calm and serene. And though it was her favorite room in the house, it was lonely. It was definitely better than being stuck outside, feeling like a fool in front of everyone when her spells backfired... which was pretty much every time.

She could never manage to execute her spells correctly. Even though the ones that she chose to try were often trivial, they all seemed to go awry. She once tried to turn a puppy into a miniature pony and ended up with a giant, angry goat. It ran around the property, knocking the other fairies down and ravaging the garden before she was able to turn it back into a dog. It was so humiliating... almost as embarrassing as her fluffy white wings.

The others' wings were so shiny and beautiful. Even the boys' wings were superior. They were massive and masculine. If her wings were out, she felt like she was leaving a trail of white feathered fluff behind her. She was just happy to have at least perfected the spell to make them disappear. Well, they didn't completely disappear; they just turned into what looked like angel wing tattoos on her back. It was very intricate, and it covered her entire back. Luckily for her, that was currently a somewhat trendy tattoo to have. That made wearing tank tops a possibility. It was pretty much the only spell that she had ever gotten right.

School work was so easy for her though, so she devoted most of her time to it. She was smart enough to ease though everything. It was a breeze. There was nothing complicated in that aspect of her life and that was a relief. It was too bad only half of her time was spent at school.

TWO

Brynn could feel the anticipation balling up in the pit of her stomach before she even stepped foot onto her property at the end of her walk home from school. She knew there was no chance of getting out of practice today. Knowing her luck, she would probably have to work extra over the weekend to make up for her slacking off during the rest of the week.

She went straight up to her room once she was in her house and changed into her training clothes. She sat down on her bed for a moment and thought about Max.

She wanted to go to the beach with him so badly. He was like a piece of forbidden fruit. She knew that she needed to stay away, despite her overwhelming desire not to. His strength and masculinity were matched only by his wit. He listened to most of the same kind of music as Brynn and even liked the same type of movies and books. That made him even better to hang out with. He always tried to make sure she was laughing or smiling. Sometimes her face even hurt from grinning by the time she made it to her next class. It was like he had been sent to her just to get her out of her doldrums. If only she could be with him in a bigger capacity.

Just like all of her other friends, she couldn't be completely honest with him about why they couldn't hang out very often. She had been able to go to his house a few times to work on school projects, but he was never invited to hers. He understood. Most people thought it would be uncomfortable to be around a very strict and religious household anyway. She doubted that anyone actually wanted an invitation. If the situation was reversed, she would be just fine not receiving an invitation to deal with that.

She tried to push those thoughts out of her head as she headed down to the grounds to unsuccessfully cast some spells. "Just get it over with. Yes, the other girls will be mean. Your spells are probably gonna suck. Nothing's gonna work out right. It is what it is. Just get it over with... and whatever you do, don't you dare cry." She repeated her mantra over and over in her head during her walk. She didn't have any inspirational Rocky type of music to play on her way to cast so this would have to do.

"It's about time you decided to come out here and pretend to contribute." Her sister Fiona snorted as she tossed her shimmery hair over her shoulder. The bright colors underneath was eye popping today.

She despised Fiona. She was everything that Brynn wasn't. She was blonde, beautiful and a powerful caster – everything that a fairy should be. Brynn just walked by her without even acknowledging the insult. What would be the point of it anyway? Responding would only make things worse. She couldn't win. She never did.

"Great comeback." Fiona mumbled to one of the other girls nearby. They all looked over their shoulders and smirked as they continued to cast. Brynn continued to do what she did best and ignored them.

She decided to try three spells that she hadn't tried before. One would make it rain rose petals, one would turn her into the size of a cat and the other one would turn a butterfly into a unicorn. She knew she would not succeed at any of them, but it would ensure that she would be out of practice in a very timely manner. Call it self-sabotage if you want, she called it working smarter not harder. She could retreat to her room and pretend that she was somewhere else... probably with Max.

That's who she usually imagined she was with when she was lost in thought. The location often changed, but Max always remained the same. Sometimes it was the beach, other times it was in the woods or somewhere nice outside. The where didn't matter. It was the company that did.

As she predicted, casting was a disaster from the start. She recited what she thought was the spell for rain and nothing happened. She stood there in the yard dumbfounded. The other girls snickered at her and whispered to each other as they continued to cast advanced spells that actually worked. She wanted to quit and go running back inside. Tears were beginning to sting her eyes, but she refused to let anyone see her cry.

After a moment, rose colored sparks began to shoot out from her fingertips. It started out slow and subtle, almost unnoticeable. Unfortunately, it escalated very quickly. She tried to conceal her fright, but it was no use. She was visibly shaking, and it was beginning to draw attention. It didn't hurt, but she was about to have a total freak out. She had no clue what she should do, and other people were beginning to panic. She closed her eyes and tried to calm herself when she got a sudden urge to lift her hands to the sky.

Once she did, her spell came to an absolute head. Brilliant pink fireworks appeared over everyone. They were breathtaking and bigger than anything she had ever seen on Independence Day. She had somehow turned her fingers into firework shooters. Fantastic. Luckily, it only lasted for a few moments before the sparks gradually retracted and she was back to normal.

"Nice job, Brynn. The whole neighborhood probably saw that. Do you want to get us all in trouble? The police could show up. How would we possibly explain all of this?" Fiona rolled her eyes at the other girls in her group and Brynn blushed as she looked away. Sweat was rolling down her forehead. She wiped her face with the back of her hand.

This sucked. She wasn't enduring this by choice, so she wished that Fiona would just leave her alone for once. Fiona had always let it be known that she thought that she was better than Brynn even though they shared the same bloodline. At least the boy fairies were nicer to her. They mostly just kept quiet and kept their distance. That was fine with her. She didn't like any of them anyway.

For her cat size spell, she didn't change her size at all. She had to admit that she was baffled when she recited the spell and just like before, nothing happened. What were the odds that it would happen two times in a row, even for her? She began to worry that she was about to see sparks again or something even worse when she felt something brush up against her leg.

She jumped at the sudden sensation. After the last display, her nerves were definitely on edge. What could that possibly be? The possibilities at this point were absolutely frightening. When she finally mustered up the nerve to look down, she saw the cutest grey striped tabby cat that she had ever seen. He rubbed his long, white whiskered face against her as he purred loudly. It sounded like he had a little motor inside of him. She leaned down and pet him as he rolled onto his back, revealing a fluffy brown belly. It was instant love. Could fairies grow up to be crazy cat ladies? That's a life she thought she could deal with.

"At least I got the cat part right." She thought to herself. She sighed audibly as she continued to pet her new feline friend and wondered if her mom would let her keep him. She decided to let him roam around the yard for a bit. His presence wouldn't harm or distract anyone enough to be a problem. One more spell to go and she could put this trying day behind her. She was so beyond ready for it to end. So, she closed her eyes, visualized one of the butterflies that were fluttering around the bright pink and orange Zinnias in the yard and delivered the spell.

When she opened her eyes, she couldn't believe what she saw. It was incredible. She actually managed to turn one of the butterflies into a magnificent unicorn. Was this a joke or something? Her eyes quickly darted around her. She was so proud of herself. It was beautiful and majestic. The silky white coat it adorned had a slight rainbow-colored tint that shined brightly in the sun. Almost like an oil slick in a puddle of water. Its horn was solid white. It stood obediently before her, looking into her eyes like it understood why it was there with her. It knelt down, as if to offer her an invitation to come aboard. She hopped onto its back and trotted around for a while. When she dismounted, she gave it a pat on the head and turned him back into his original butterfly form.

None of the other fairies said a word,

although all eyes were currently on her. Of course, they didn't have the decency to say anything nice when she actually got something right. It didn't matter though. She just rode her on conjured unicorn, and nobody could take that away from her. She dusted herself off and pompously marched inside. She didn't care if it was just one spell. It was enough... especially for her. The still presently spellbound cat followed closely behind her, making its way into the fairy house.

Her whole fairy family lived together. So as one would imagine, their home was very sizeable. It looked like a castle. Well, it was a like a modern castle really... not like the castle's you think of from the days of kings and queens. It was three stories high, made of dark red brick and was covered in vines and greenery. It was set far back in the woods, giving it extra protection and seclusion. The whole property was surrounded by a ten-foot wooden privacy fence. It was on twenty acres of land and the house itself was about 15,000 square feet. It had to be that big, though. There were at least twenty people scurrying around at any one time. Often there would be more. The last thing needed with that many personalities was a bunch of shared bathrooms and bedrooms. They were lucky to be able to have such a comfortable living space.

It was more skill than luck, though. One of the perks that came with being magical was wealth. Their specials gifts allowed them to afford to live the way they did. Everyone on the outside attributed it to contributions from people who supported their crazy religious cult. It wasn't a good thing for people to think, but it was safer for them to think that rather than the truth.

It was part of their job as an adult fairy to keep up that persona. They learned how to charm people into doing things for them and that usually involved money or items of great value. This encompassed a wide array of schemes ranging from winning the lottery and acquiring prized possessions, to landing lucrative jobs.

Brynn was happy to have one more year before she had to deal with any of that. For now, she would enjoy human high school and her youth. Once it was gone, she knew the responsibilities that would await her were significant.

THREE

Brynn's weekend was incredibly dull. In fact, the only thing that got her through it at all was the thought of seeing Max at school on Monday. She didn't even know if he liked her the same way that she liked him, but it didn't really matter. She wasn't allowed to date human boys anyway. He was just someone to give her hope and that was all that was relevant right now. It was enough for her. But today something was off.

Max seemed distant, like he was either mad at her or just avoiding her all together. She assumed that he must still be mad at her for not joining him at the beach on Friday. He would just have to get over it. She would have very happily gone with him if it would have been a possibility for her. If really given a choice, she would always choose him. Always. No questions about it. So, she did what any non-confrontational girl would do in that situation and tried to stay away from him for the rest of the day until he cooled down.

Lunch was boring without him, but she survived. She saw him come into the cafeteria and get a slice of pizza but didn't see where he went after that. She couldn't keep from gazing around the lunchroom as she ate her turkey and provolone cheese sub sandwich that she brought from home for the majority of the time. He must have gone outside to eat his food. Pretty immature.

He kept his nose buried in textbooks during the classes they shared. As soon as class was dismissed, he was a ghost again. And when there were only ten minutes left in the last period of the day, she was glad that this little game was over. She didn't know what his problem was with any certainty, but she was positive that it would be drama that she didn't want to deal with. She had enough dramatic people around her at home to bring her down. The bell finally rang, and she grabbed her bag and walked into the hallway.

She had barely made it out of the classroom when someone lightly grabbed her by the arm. She spun around hurriedly, expecting one of Fiona's cronies to be messing with her, but saw Max standing there holding her in place. It took her by surprise. She hadn't seen him for most of the day and he didn't talk to her when they were in classes together. She assumed that she was in the clear at this point.

"Hey. Sorry I've been weird all day. Do you think we could hang out a little before you go home? I'd really like to spend some time with you since we didn't get a chance to hang out on Friday." His body language was awkward and hard to read. He was definitely avoiding eye contact with her. It wasn't like he had tried to talk to her at all today. Why now? Was he lying to her? If only she had some of that fairy charm right about now.

She really didn't know what to think. She did have time though. Everyone was so impressed that her spell actually worked on Friday that they were all being a bit lax with her training schedule. Scared she was making the wrong decision, but not willing to turn down any alone time with Max, she agreed to hang out.

"I can hang for a little bit. What do you wanna do?" she asked, trying hard to read his expression. It was no use, though. His face may well have been made of stone. He would make an excellent poker player.

"It's such a nice day outside. Why don't we go to the park? I can drive us." He continued to avoid eye contact with her as he turned and began walking out of school. It was not going unnoticed. Something was definitely off.

She followed him out to the parking lot and hopped into his car. There were a few parks close enough to walk to, but he wanted to go to one near his house. She had no objections to that. There were usually less people at that park. It would just mean more alone time with him and less of a chance of seeing anyone that she knew. Being alone in the park with a human would be a tough one to explain.

The drive there was quiet and awkward. Brynn thought that it was mostly in her head, but Max felt the same way. She knew something was wrong with him earlier in the day and he knew that he did a terrible job of hiding it. She was still mentally obsessing about it in the passenger seat. Nevertheless, she was itching to get outside in the fresh air. The whole ride had been painfully silent, and it took all she had not to jump out of the car the second that they pulled into a parking space. The wheels were almost still moving when she opened her car door.

"So, what do you have in mind now that we are here?" she asked, finally breaking the silence.

"There is a gazebo close by. Let's go hang out in there." He still wasn't looking at her. His gaze was fixed to the ground in front of him. Was he guilty of something? They were just friends, so it couldn't be about some sort of betrayal. He owed her nothing.

Brynn anxiously followed him to the gazebo and took a seat beside him on one of the inside benches. It was hot outside, but the ceiling fan in the top of the gazebo created a much-needed cool breeze. She would be happy when cooler weather arrived, she thought to herself. She hated to sweat and with Max there with her, she was very aware of how much she was perspiring. These southern summers could be absolutely brutal.

"Look, I brought you here for a reason Brynn." Max said abruptly, finally making eye contact with her. He was nervous, but he told himself to just get over it and do what he was there to do. Putting it off was only making the anxiety build up inside of him.

Her heart, as well as her mind, began to race. She felt the blood drain out of her face and he paused a moment before speaking again. She had to be as white as a ghost right now.

He chuckled for a second then rubbed his hands on his face and through his hair. He was nervous.

"This is completely ridiculous, and I can't even believe I'm saying it out loud. Whatever. I'm just gonna get if off my chest and then we can have a laugh about it or something." He made a long sigh that sounded like a mix of nervousness and exasperation. "I really can't believe I am saying this. Brynn... I know what you are."

Panic.

Those were the words she had always dreaded hearing and she didn't know what to do now that she actually was. She felt like her heart was going to beat out of her chest entirely. Everything was starting to spin. She knew what he had to be talking about. She was a fairy. There wasn't any other big secret that she was hiding. She couldn't confess anything, though. What if she was wrong? Maybe he was playing some sort of stupid joke. She couldn't risk the punishment she'd receive just because she was being paranoid. That would look great. Throwing out an "I'm a fairy" confession when he was planning on saying "You're a great friend" would be more than a misstep.

"What are you talking about?" she tried to

chuckle, hoping to laugh it off, but failed miserably in her attempt. If anyone was acting guilty of something, it was definitely her at this point. She made a mental note to never play poker.

"I followed you home on Friday. I didn't believe the bullshit reason you gave me for not being able to go to the beach. Something just told me you were lying to me. I just knew it. I wanted to know what the truth was. So, I went to your house and snuck around the guards. You were never going to tell me the truth. That was the only way I was going to find out. I watched you and the others through a crack in the fence."

"What do you think you saw?" she asked quietly, still not wanting to accept the fact that her worst fear was being confirmed but knowing exactly what he had to have seen. She chose her wording carefully. Asking what he *thought* he saw left a possibility that he was wrong.

"I saw you... cast spells or something. I saw your sister shrink down to a ridiculously small size and fly around. Brynn, I saw you riding a unicorn. A UNICORN! Do you know how ridiculous this is to say out loud? I feel like I am stuck in some crazy, far out there sci-fi movie. How does this make any sense?" His voice was beginning to get a bit loud. Frantic, even. It was a good thing the park was so empty.

She didn't even have a response. There was nothing that she could say to make it seem better than it was, and she couldn't deny the things that he had seen. It all happened on Friday, just like he said. How was she going to convince him that he didn't see what he clearly had?

"You are a fairy or something, right? That is the only thing that somehow makes sense." He laughed in his head at his statement. How could that possibly make sense? He started rubbing his face again. He felt like he was stuck in a weird dream. These types of things weren't supposed to be real.

"Yes, I am a fairy." Her response was so quiet it could barely qualify as a whisper. She decided that her only option was to fess up. What else could she do at this point? She would lose him otherwise. That couldn't happen. Please don't let this backfire.

"My family comes from a very long line of fair folk. We let people talk about us being religious to hide the bigger truth, because it is dangerous for people to know about us and what we are." She was still talking quietly and still hadn't made eye contact with him. She felt more like an outcast than ever before right now.

"So, what does that entail? Do you fly around tricking people and stealing babies? That's what I read online when I typed the word 'fairy' into a search engine."

Brynn laughed out loud, thankful for Max's sense of humor and naivety. It broke up the awkwardness a bit.

"That is what folklore nonsense is made of. Yes, we are magical and by nature a bit mischievous, but most of what you read online is untrue. Humans have quite active imaginations it turns out. A simple thought or suggestion from someone can turn into cold hard fact in the blink of an eye as far as most are concerned."

Max was silent a moment, trying to take it all in. It was one thing to think that Brynn was a fairy, but it was quite another to hear her admit it. A few days ago, he didn't think anything like this even existed.

"How do you become a fairy? I assume you are born into it, but how did you guys even come to be?"

"The legends say that our race was once Angels. They were cast out of the Heavens for not being pure enough. They weren't evil enough for Hell, so they were left to roam the Earth."

"So, can you die or are you immortal? Do you age like humans or faster? Wait, are you really eighteen? Like a human kind of eighteen?"

"First of all, I'm not a secret old lady or something. I really am eighteen, as in I have only been alive for eighteen years. And yes, we can die. We do typically have longer lifespans than humans, though."

"I can't lie," Max began "this is all a bit overwhelming. Last week I thought you were just an ordinary girl with a big group of weird, bitchy relatives. Maybe even like a rebel agnostic in a family of a strict religion or something. Not this, though."

"Please, promise me you won't tell anyone what you know." Brynn began to cry. For the first time in her life, she was scared about her family secret getting out. She had never understood the seriousness of it all until right now. There could be real and harsh consequences for both of them. It was hitting her like a ton of bricks. How could she be so naïve?

"I won't say anything to anybody Brynn. You should know that. Come on. Just don't lie to me about anything else. Please. I really like you a lot. You can trust me, and I'd like to think that I could trust you as well."

"No lies. I promise." Brynn said as she tried to wipe the tears from her eyes. She was a bit embarrassed that she had let herself get so emotional. How was it possible that he was being so cool about all of this? Most people would be running for the hills right now. She wasn't even going into the details about not being able to tell him a lie. He didn't need all of the fairy particulars right now.

"A fairy girlfriend I can deal with, but not

a liar."

Girlfriend?

She smiled as Max reached for her hand and held it in his. What was happening right now? He was more upset that she hadn't been upfront with him than he was about her being a fairy. This had been a total emotional roller coaster.

Her heart skipped at the thought of being his girlfriend though. It was highly illegal in the fairy realm, but it made her so happy at the moment. He was all that she had been desiring since he entered her life. Not just because he was nice to look at, either. He was smart, intriguing, and different than the other humans. He had a beautiful mind. Right now, she felt like Eve, and he was a juicy honey crisp apple.

He was all that she wanted. Forbidden or not.

They sat in silence for a little while. He was content just sitting there with Brynn's head on his shoulder. They had both been wanting this for so long. Neither of them even realized the feeling was mutual until today.

The circumstances that made it happen were unexpected for sure, but they were happy now. She didn't want the moment to end, but she knew her mom would have it in for her if she stayed out for much longer. It could pique someone's interest for sure.

They walked back to Max's car hand in hand. She gave him a hug goodbye and opted to walk home to not raise suspicions. The sun was beginning to set, and the sky was a beautiful mix of pink and orange. The clouds were a bluish shade of purple and looked almost like smoke against the bright sky. The temperature had dropped a bit, but it was still quite balmy. She could smell the fragrant honeysuckles in the bushes lining the sidewalk. This was the kind of evening she would enjoy if she didn't have the fact that she just spilled her family's secret looming over her. She wished she could just soak up the scenery and the thought of her new closeness with Max without having to stress about other things.

When she got home, she quickly washed up and joined everyone for dinner. She was completely paranoid through the rest of the night. She sat awkwardly through the meal, worried someone would ask where she had gone after school at any moment. Good thing she was pretty awkward during their conversations already. Maybe no one would notice if she began to stumble over her words. She would have made up a story to cover for what she was doing, but fairies were unable to lie. It would be no use for her to even try. So as soon as she cleared her plate of food, she asked to be excused to go start working on her homework. She had never been so thankful to have assignments to do than she was right now.

Making people aware that you were a fairy was a major deal in her world. It is one of the first things fairy children are taught in fact. If you were caught revealing the truth, you could actually be exiled. They were all told stories when they were younger of times when the cat got out of the bag. If the elders were willing to cut all ties and banish a family member because of it, she shuttered at the thought of what would happen to the commoners that were told about the fae. They never heard about what happened to them. Common sense just told them that the elders wouldn't stand for someone who knew about them being free to roam around the world to potentially speak of what they knew. It just wasn't going to happen. That risk was far too large to take.

The last fairy to tell the family secret was Brynn's aunt Madeleine. She wasn't spoken of much, not even by her mother. She didn't know if that was due to sadness or to fear. Madeleine fell in love with a human boy when they were about Brynn's age, and she confessed her heritage to him one night. She thought that it would be okay for him to know about her life because she intended on marrying and starting a family with him. She had dreams that were bigger than the fairy world. That kind of activity with humans was forbidden, though. The elders said they would not tolerate any of her foolish plans and they took her away in the middle of the night. She was never seen or heard from again. It was almost as if she had never even existed. Brynn learned the story when she was young. It was especially alarming because it happened to someone close to her. She would ask her mother about it from time to time, but she would always change the subject. There were so many unanswered questions.

That story was all that Brynn could think

about while she was lying in bed that night. Sleep was definitely going to be evading her. She would never be able to forgive herself if something happened to Max because she was careless. It was a matter of being in the wrong place at the wrong time. She was to blame regardless. There is a reason that her kind didn't have human friends, and this was it. She never fully grasped the magnitude of what she was keeping concealed until now. She should have been more careful.

FOUR

Hiding the danger that Max was potentially in wasn't fair to him. He deserved to know what he had gotten himself into. Another trip to the park was in order so they could discuss what his newfound knowledge meant. The park really was the safest place to have such a conversation. This whole situation wasn't as simple as he might have been thinking. So,

Brynn spent the morning getting ready for school and trying to figure out exactly what to say to him.

It was early, but it was already hot and humid outside. She took her usual stance more than several feet behind the others on her walk to school. She enjoyed the solitude that the fog brought. It was so thick that it made her feel like she was by herself and not close to the other stuck-up fairies. She could just disappear in the thickness.

"Hey beautiful." Max greeted Brynn with a smile as she arrived at school. She tried to push her nervousness aside and act normal. That wasn't an issue for very long. He gave her a hug and that anxiety was instantly replaced with giddiness. He smelled so good, like cologne and fresh laundry. It could be so easy to get lost in him and forget all of her complications. If only that were a viable option.

"Do you have plans after class today?" she asked excitedly. It was almost as if she had forgotten why she needed to talk to him. Right now, a part of her just wanted to be alone with him.

"I have nothing going on that's more important than you. What did you have in mind?" He could sense that she was nervous about something, but he didn't ask what it was. If it was important, she would tell him. After their talk in the park yesterday, he truly believed that. People lie and make mistakes, but that doesn't mean that they will make the wrong choice repeatedly. Everyone deserves a second chance.

"I was hoping that we could go to the park and hang out for a little while before I have to be home."

"That sounds great." He said as he gave her a kiss on the cheek. She could feel electricity run through her. She smiled as they walked to class together. She couldn't help it. He was all she wanted. Max made her felt normal... or as normal as she could be.

She knew it was dangerous to show Max any type of affection in public. If any of the other fairies saw, there would be some definite questions raised. For now, though, she didn't care. Max was filling a hole in her heart and that felt great. She finally felt like she had someone totally on her team. Besides, after their talk after school today, he may not want to give her affection anymore. She needed to soak it up while she could. He had a choice to make.

Brynn was so preoccupied with going to the park that her classes passed by fairly quickly. She had no clue what had been discussed in any of them, though. Hopefully, the homework wouldn't throw her for too much of a loop because of it. She found herself almost shaking with nervous energy when the bell rang after the last period.

"Are you ready to go?" Max met her at the doorway of her last class. She nodded with a smile, and they walked to his car. She glanced around to make sure no fairies saw her.

They made small chit chat on the way to the park. It was mostly about how their classes had been and the songs on the radio. They agreed on most of them, but she was definitely more into pop music than he was. There was more rap in his list of favorite songs. When they pulled into the parking lot, she suggested that they head over to the gazebo again. He followed closely behind her, lightly grazing his fingertips back and forth across her back. It felt nice.

"I did bring you back here for a reason." She said to him as they each took a seat on the bench. It seemed like all of their outings were starting out that way now. Her tone must have sounded serious enough because he turned to face her and gave her his full attention.

"We need to talk about your life now that you know about me. There is a lot that I didn't tell you yesterday."

"Like what?" Max asked, definitely skeptical of what Brynn was beginning to tell him. Who cared that she was different?

"There have only been a few humans that have known about us over time. The last fairy to let the secret slip was my mom's sister Madeleine back when she was seventeen. When the elders found out, they banished her. None of us have ever heard what happened to the guy. We haven't heard from Madeleine since. We assume that she is living a 'human' life somewhere, but to my knowledge no one really knows.

Max just sat there in silence. Brynn didn't

even give him a chance to talk before she started to cry. The magnitude of their situation was becoming overwhelming.

"I'm so sorry to put you in harm's way." She sobbed into his shoulder, her heart breaking. "I don't know what might happen to you if they find out what you know. I shouldn't have been your friend. I should have just stayed away." She was crying so much at this point that she felt hysterical. It was hard to catch her breath.

"Look at me, Brynn. You didn't do anything wrong. I made the choice to go to your house and spy on you. That's on me. If you had known that I was going to do that, you would have found a way to stop me. You wouldn't risk it. Please stop crying babe." He put his hand to her face and wiped her tears. His heart broke at the sight of her sadness. He felt like this was all his fault. If he hadn't gone to spy on her she wouldn't be a mess right now. He just wanted to know the truth about her. She was special. He knew that even before he saw what she could do.

"Well, I think we should make a choice right now. Either we go our separate ways and stay safe, or we find a way to hide this. I understand if you choose option one. There is still a chance for you. There is no reason for you to be risking your life for me." Brynn said quietly. "It doesn't make sense. You could easily find a new girl to be friends with. There are plenty of girls at our school that would jump at the opportunity."

Max cupped his hands around her face softly.

"Don't you realize how special you are? And not because you are a fairy, but because of how you make me feel. I don't care what you are telling me right now. I would risk it all for you. I knew that from the second I saw your face on my first day at school. So, let's start thinking about solutions, because suggesting that I walk away from you is absolutely insane."

All Brynn could do was smile as Max wiped away more tears from her rosy cheeks. This whole time he had felt it too.

"I don't even know where to start thinking."

"How about we start with your aunt?

Maybe we can find a way to track her down and talk to her. Surely *someone* must know where she is. People disappear all the time, but it is very rarely without a trace."

"Max, I have tried to ask my mom about her many, many times. She will never say a single word. She always changes the subject."

"Well, maybe that's the problem. Sometimes actions speak louder than words and you have to take things into your own hands. Find a new approach."

"What, like snoop around or something?"

"Didn't you tell me that fairies are a bit mischievous? I extremely doubt that character trait doesn't apply to you." He grinned, knowing it was the truth.

"I suppose you are right. I can poke around at home and see what I come up with. As long as I am careful with my timing it should be fine. I will try to look around tonight. I'll have a better chance if I get home and look while everyone is still outside."

"Let's get going then. You can text me whenever and let me know if you find something worth noting. They don't monitor your phone or anything, do they?"

"No, they would never have to do anything like that. If they ever had a suspicion, they would just need to ask."

"What do you mean? Wouldn't they just assume that you would be lying to them? Are fairies just really trusting?"

"Oh, I guess there are some things that I forget that you don't already know. Fairies can't tell a lie. We can be vague and dance around the question, but not just outright untruthful. That's why they would just have to ask. I would spill the beans."

"Well, that's pretty damn inconvenient. Please try not to act suspiciously then." Max laughed, but Brynn knew that he wasn't kidding. He was anxious.

He dropped her off close enough to her house to get there quickly, but far enough away that no one would see. While she couldn't lie, she could omit things. If anyone were to ask where she had been, she would just say that she was at the park. She made her way through the guard post at the front of the property and went through the gate. Everyone was outside casting spells, so she tried to casually walk to the house. She said hello to her mother who was in the kitchen cooking and went upstairs.

She tossed her backpack on her neatly made bed. She knew that the one spell that could help her in her endeavor was a shrinking spell. She watched the others cast it all the time. She had tried it once before and failed, but she had to try it again now. She stood in the middle of her room and tried to concentrate when she felt her phone vibrate.

"Good luck. <3!" was on the screen.

"Thanks for the well wishes, Max." She thought to herself as she closed her eyes and focused, hoping to not accidentally turn into a giant. She began to cast the spell and could feel herself shrink as soon as she said the last word. She was so excited that she had cast another spell correctly, but she had no time to celebrate. There was work to be done.

She slipped into the hallway and did a bit of recon. There was no one to be seen anywhere nearby, so she ducked into her mom's bedroom. Brynn knew her mom was cooking, but she still wanted to move with haste. She could not let anyone catch her in her mom's room.

She figured that if there was any information to be found, it would be in her dresser drawers, so she started there. Luckily, she didn't make herself small enough that the drawers would be too heavy for her to open and navigate. The top two drawers contained nothing but socks and panties. It was just tank tops and pajamas in the middle two. She opened the bottom two drawers and found a gold mine of papers. She started browsing page by page, but quickly realized that would take far too long. There was so much there. She would be caught long before she found anything good. She put her hands at the very bottom of the stack, lifted up the papers and took a peek. Anything worth hiding wouldn't be in plain sight.

She was looking for anything that looked different or out of place. There, in the back corner, were two small pink envelopes. She pulled one out and checked the front. It had a return address, but no name. She took a picture of the address with her phone. She was going to open the envelope and see what was inside, but she could hear someone coming up the stairs. She quickly put everything back as she had found it and hid in the corner of the room. Hopefully that address will be enough. The footsteps went past the bedroom, and she breathed a sigh of relief. She couldn't risk staying in there any longer. The anxiety might just kill her. She slipped out and returned to her own bedroom.

She closed the door quickly behind her. She stood there for a few minutes with her back pressed up against the door. What an adrenaline rush. She took a deep breath and tried to steady herself. Her heart was beating so fast. That could have ended so badly.

She had no idea if this was the address that she was looking for, but it was all she had to go on. She sent Max a text message with the address and asked him to look into it. Just to be safe, she deleted the message and the picture that she took. There was no such thing as being too careful around the compound. Those spiteful bitches would stop at nothing to get her into trouble. Her phone wasn't being monitored, but she couldn't trust anyone around there. Maybe her mom, but no one else. Certainly not Fiona.

It was getting close to dinner time, so she took a quick shower before heading downstairs. Maybe that would give her time to refresh and not look so guilty. Anything could help, right? After she threw on some comfy clothes, she went down to the kitchen to join her family.

Luckily for her, it was like most nights around there. Bustling. It was pot roast night, so most were busy scarfing food. Her mom's pot roast could win an award. It was her specialty. She paired it with smashed potatoes and gravy, carrots, green beans, and homemade biscuits. There were about twenty fairies sitting around the table., mostly uninterested in conversation. Thank God.

Someone asked her how school was and if her homework was finished, but other than that no one paid any attention to her. Well, other than Fiona. He found plenty of opportunities to throw some insults her way. She didn't respond to any of them. It made it easier in situations like these. No need to worry about getting caught when no one cared, she thought to herself. It was what it was.

FIVE

"Were you able to find anything on that address that I sent you last night?" Brynn asked Max as they made their way to first period.

"I looked it up online last night. It wasn't as fruitful as I hoped it would be. I couldn't find a name to go with it, but I saved the directions on how to get there. I don't suppose you would be able to get away long enough to go with me, would you? It could be a fun adventure."

"Today? You know that I can't. Are you sure you are willing to go there? There is no telling who that address even belongs to. You could be going on a wild goose chase or something worse. The address is from a fairy... a whole other set of rules apply here babe. I don't think it's safe. Let's give it a little more time to come up with a better plan." They sat down at their table and Max sighed.

"Trust me, this is the only way. There has to be a way to help us, and I am gonna figure it out. If I don't go tonight, I will just sit at home and play video games. That's lame. I can't choose laziness over us. I want to be able to tell the whole world that you are mine, Brynn. It's something I have wanted from my first day at this school." He grabbed her hand and held it tightly under the table. Her heart fluttered wildly and as their fingers interlaced. She knew that he was right. They had to find a way. Quickly.

Brynn was excited at the possibility of Max getting answers, but she was scared at the same time. She couldn't shake the feeling she was getting that something bad was in the works. She hoped that she was just being paranoid because it wouldn't make a difference to him anyway. He wasn't going to change his mind now. She knew that he was going regardless of the bad feeling she had. Guys could be so stubborn. She just wished that there was someone who could go with him. He needed to have backup. She couldn't tell anyone else her secret, though. It was already putting Max in jeopardy. One endangered person was more than enough.

They discussed what he would say if he found Madeleine in his search during their classes. He was planning to leave right after school, so they wouldn't have another chance to talk. Ugh, this was all happening so fast. Too fast. She thought they'd have more time. She didn't like jumping into anything without a plan. It was too stressful.

Brynn jotted down a list of things she needed him to talk to Madeleine about. She knew that he would be fine on his own, but she couldn't leave anything out. This could be their one and only shot at getting answers. Ever. She needed to know what really happened to Madeleine's boyfriend. Was she really able to blend into human society and live a semi-normal life? What were their genuine risks? How many of the rumors she had heard growing up were real and not just embellished bullshit?

When the final bell rang, her heart sank. She caught a glimpse of Max in the parking lot as he was getting into his car. He gave her a quick wink and smile, but then he was gone. She choked back the giant lump in her throat and began to walk home. She turned on the discman she was thankful to have since she couldn't have music on her phone, popped in her earbuds and tried to tune everything else out on her walk. She couldn't show up in tears. She would cast a spell on herself if she thought it were even worth trying. Realistically, she would just muck it up and feel worse about things afterward.

Thank God she skipped out on her chores and duties around the house so far this week. She had no protests to training today. There was nothing else for her to do and this was her chance to keep her mom in her good graces. In the event that anything she and Max were trying were to go awry, she would need her mom on her side. If she could just get a spell right today, she could lay low again for a few days if need be.

The more spells she tried, the better her chances of getting one right had to be. So, she decided to do as many spells as it took. Her first one was the shrinking spell that she had done the day before. She was sure that she could get that one right again and she was correct about that. Once she started to cast, she was itty bity in no time at all.

"One down." She thought to herself, feeling quite a bit more amped. It wasn't often that she was able to feel confident while casting.

She kept doing spell after spell and she was nailing every single one of them. She didn't know what had come over her. It had to be the emotions that she was feeling about Max. She was never this fired up. It was the only thing that was different from every other time she practiced. She took a look around her and noticed that everyone had stopped casting their own spells. Their eyes were all on her. It made her feel even more empowered. She wanted them all, especially Fiona, to eat their words.

"Well, well, what has come over you, my girl?" She turned quickly to see her mom standing there, hands on her hips, admiring her handiwork.

"I don't know." She said with a chuckle. "I guess I just got tired of everyone making me feel like a jackass." It was partially true. No need to bring up the Max factor.

"Whatever it takes, Brynn. You're doing a great job. Come on inside and get washed up for dinner."

She followed behind her mom, trying not to smile too much. She didn't know what she was happier about, her spell success or her mom's rarely seen encouragement. Either way, this was a good day. It would be even better once she heard from Max. She was excited that she was going to have a chance to brag to someone about how well her spells had gone for once.

Her mom had dinner under wraps, so she showered and went downstairs to eat as soon as she was finished. It was hard not to pick at her food considering how nervous her stomach was. Thank God no one in her family was clairvoyant. She couldn't think about anything but Max and what he might find out about Madeleine. She excused herself pretty early and went to her room. Her day had been successful enough that no one gave her a hard time.

She was so worried that she hadn't heard from Max yet. That had to mean that he was having an intense conversation with Madeleine. At least that was what she kept telling herself. She sat in bed for hours waiting to hear from him until she finally fell asleep.

When her phone chirped at three in the morning, it startled her awake. She rolled over to grab her phone and check the message. It was from Max. Her pulse was already kicking into high gear.

"I forgot to ask you something very important when we were in the park."

"What?" she replied, feeling very confused and sleepy. That wasn't the message she was expecting to see.

"If fairies exist, then what other

supernatural things are out there? What else is real?"

"Max you aren't making any sense. Are you okay??" She didn't know if it was him or just her still being half asleep. Something was off, though. Why was he being so cryptic? She just needed him to say if the mission was a success or failure.

"I need to see you now. How can we make that happen?"

Max seemed serious, so she decided to risk it. He knew what the stakes would be for her to leave at this time of night. He wouldn't ask if it wasn't important. She cast the shrinking spell on herself once again and slipped out of her bedroom window. Being super small makes you very light on your feet, so she sailed off of her balcony and to the ground with no problem. It was kind of exhilarating.

They agreed to meet at their usual spot in the park, so she headed off in that direction. She snuck through the crack in the fence that Max had watched her through. If no one had fixed that crack yet, she knew they wouldn't notice her leaving through it tonight. They probably didn't even know it was there.

Max was sitting in the gazebo when she got there. He was dressed in jeans and a black hoodie pulled down over part of his face. It was a little more emo looking that he usually dressed which definitely piqued her curiosity. He very rarely had anything covering his hair. It was one of his best features.

He said nothing as she made her way to him.

"Are you okay?" she yelled out as she got a bit closer, but there was still no word from him. The unusually crisp summer breeze swept by her, sending a chill down her back. She shivered for a brief moment. His strange behavior was beginning to scare her, and she was getting nervous.

"Hey?" she said as she stepped into the gazebo. "What the hell is wro..." she trailed off.

Max looked up at her and he didn't have to say a word. She understood what the urgency and the strange behavior was about. His olive skin was much paler now than it was when she said goodbye to him at school. His lips were rosy, and his already golden eyes were now an absolutely brilliant shade.

"Who did this to you?" she choked out in barely a whisper.

"I take it you know what has happened to me then. I don't know his name. When I asked him why he was doing it, he said it was for Fiona. Do you know what that could mean? I don't even know anyone named Fiona." His bottom lip had blood marks on it from where his fangs must have come out for the first time. He looked youthful and fatigued at the same time somehow. How could this have happened?

Brynn was dumbfounded. She just stood there in disbelief. Her sister had done this to him. It dawned on her that she had been very careful never to mention any of the other fairy girls' names to him. It was for his own protection. He had no idea who her sister was. He couldn't just be making that part up.

"Earth to Brynn... did you hear me?" he asked, snapping her back to reality. He had such an attitude right now, but who could blame him? His life had just been changed drastically and permanently. "Why the fuck did this happen to me?"

"Fiona is my sister." She couldn't say any more than that. She didn't know what *to* say. The blank expression on her face didn't give justice to the swarm of emotions she was feeling. This was all her fault. She should have gone with him... she knew it would be dangerous. Why did she have to ignore the bad feeling that she had? His life was ruined now because of her.

"Why the hell would your sister want to do this to me? Does she even know who I am?" His voice was curt. The anger was just seeping out of him.

"I don't know!" Brynn cried out, feeling desperate. "I never even talk to my sister. She's a bitch. How could she know who you are?"

"She must not want us to be together. This will work out well for her then. Now that I am a freak of the night, I don't know when I can even see you. I definitely can't go to school. Not unless I am feeling a bit suicidal.

God only knows what I am going to tell my parents. This isn't something that I can just explain away."

"Tell me exactly what happened to you."

"I never made it to the address you gave me. I was getting close. It's over in that nice neighborhood that's at the edge of our school district. It had just started getting dark. Something ran out in front of the car. I thought I missed it, but it felt like I ran something over. I pulled over to see what it was. I was afraid that it was a person because it felt pretty large.

Once I made it to the passenger side, this guy was on me. I didn't even have a chance to react. The pain was intense. Once the pain stopped, I don't know. It felt like a weird bond with this guy. I tried asking him questions. He just said what he said about Fiona. He told me to get back in my care and make it home and indoors before the sun came up or I would be a goner."

"He didn't give you his name?"

"No. It all seemed to happen so fast. It feels like a dream. A bad fucking dream."

"Max, I am so sorry. This is all my fault. I should have just tried harder to mislead you. If I stopped being your friend, you would be ok."

"It's my fault. I insisted on going alone. What am I going to do now, though?"

"Let me do some research. I will figure something out, Max. I promise. But right now, I am going to get some answers. You have to make sure you get home before the sun rises. It won't be safe once the first sun beams peek out from the horizon. Even that could be too much sun for you."

She wanted to kiss him goodbye, but she didn't know if that was a good idea. He had to be thirsty. She had never met a vampire before. She knew that they existed, of course. They were all taught when they were young that there were other mystical beings out there. They were referred to as mystica. Vampires were said to be the most dangerous of them all. They were driven by desire and could be unpredictable. Fairies were taught that vampires were undead children of the night and were to be feared. She was too angry right now to be afraid of Max. She just sat there next to him, staring into those blazing eyes.

He took her in his arms and kissed her anyway. It must've taken great strength for him to do that. She could feel a slight tremble in his icy touch. The iron taste of his lips was startling, but it made the reality of the situation sink in so much more for her.

"Be careful Brynn and call me if you are in any trouble. I can be there in the blink of an eye now. I don't care what they do, nothing is going to keep us apart." He winked at her, and he was gone.

She wished that she could get home as quickly as him. She raced home as hastily as she could and made a beeline for Fiona's room once she was there. When she walked in, Fiona was sitting on the cushions set in her bay window that overlooked the garden.

"Do you have something to say to me?" Brynn stood by the door; her fists clenched.

"I assume you are referring to your baby vampire boyfriend?"

Brynn wanted to slap the smirk right off of

her face.

"How the hell did you even know about him?"

"I saw you lurking around mom's room. I cast an invisibility spell on myself so I could watch you. You were clearly up to something. I saw you rifle through her drawers, take a picture of the letters and text it to him. I wrote down the address when you left, and I called in a favor to a friend." She sat there on the windowsill acting proud of her superior self.

"Why would you do that? Was it just to torture me? You just couldn't stand the thought of me being happy, could you? Was the thought of me having a boyfriend too much or was it finally having successful spell casting that pushed you over the edge? Why do you have to be such a bitch?"

"Get a clue, Brynn. First of all, just because I don't like you doesn't mean I am an asshole. Maybe I say mean things to you, but it is what it is. You are older than me, so I have to work harder to show you up. I want to be first in line. Second, think about everything we have learned. Humans can't know about our existence. Max isn't a human anymore, is he? Doesn't that solve your fucking problem?"

Brynn sat on the edge of Fiona's bright pink bed, a bit dumbfounded. She had a point. Mystica all knew about each other already. They wouldn't have to worry about him knowing everything if he already knew it. Still, the elders wouldn't like them being together. This whole situation was giving her a headache. She got up to leave the room.

"I'm sorry I jumped to conclusions, Fiona. I'm sure you can see why I would do that. You have never done anything nice for me in the past. I don't know if Max will feel better about this or not, but thank you, I guess. I still don't know if I trust what you are saying now or not either."

"I think he will see the good in this eventually. And Brynn? If he is having trouble with sunlight, do some spell research. You might find a solution. If you can actually figure it out for once. Goodnight."

Could she not include an insult in every comment? What a bitch.

Brynn closed the door and headed to her

own bedroom. She was comforted in one way, but so confused in another. Why would Fiona do anything to benefit her? Was she just full of crap right now or was she being genuine? It was hard to even know how to tell. All she had ever done was cut Brynn down, even when they were small children. This was definitely the last thing she expected to be dealing with tonight. She knew he shouldn't have gone alone.

She tried to think about everything she had learned about vampires over the years. She knew that they were technically dead. They could go out only in the darkness and they could draw extra power from other mystica when they consumed their blood. She thought about what Fiona said about researching spells. There must be one that would help Max go out in the sunlight. Tomorrow was Saturday, so she would spend the day in the library researching spells since there was no school. For now, she would try to get some sleep after sending a quick message to Max.

"I think I can help you with the sunlight debacle. Meet me at the park tomorrow night as soon as it gets dark enough."

SIX

As the dawn's early light began to peek through her bedroom window, Brynn woke up. She hoped that Max had made it home safely before the sun started to rise. It would be convenient for him that his room was already in the basement. That would surely be the safest place for him to sleep in his house. The hardest part would be avoiding his parents. How do you explain to your parents that you are a vampire now? "Hey mom and dad, the fables are true. I survive on blood now. Oh, and my girlfriend is a fairy." No way.

She dressed quickly in jeans and an old tank top and grabbed an apple and granola bar from the kitchen on her way out of the house. She headed straight to the library. There would be other fairies there studying today, so she would have to be careful not to attract much attention to herself. The last thing that she needed was prying eyes. She didn't know where to even start looking, but Fiona's cryptic message told her that there was definitely something to be found.

She cast a quick clarity spell on herself once she was in the library. She hoped that the extra focus would help her with the task at hand. "May I think clearly and remain steadfast." She thought silently. She stood before a wall of books and closed her eyes to concentrate.

"What kind of book would a spell like this even be in?" she asked herself as she brushed her hand over the books in front of her. She closed her eyes and let her fingers linger on each binding. Some of them felt so dusty. They must not have been read in quite a while. There was so much history on the shelves.

When she opened her eyes, her hand was resting on a book of healing. Taking it as a potential sign from above, she grabbed the book and headed for a chair. Vampires were supposedly damned, so Max did have the potential to need to be healed. That made sense. Right? Just as Brynn was of angelic descent, Max was now of demonic descent. That was why the sunlight burned him. He was too impure to be in the presence of the light.

Brynn scoured the book for what must have been hours. There were so many pages. She was being so careful not to miss anything that could be useful, so it took a while to go from page to page. She had officially learned how to heal every type of human, mystica, and fairy ailment that existed, but nothing for vampires. There were only ten pages left to read and she wanted to scream out loud in frustration. This felt impossible. She took a deep breath and turned though the last few pages. There was nothing there that could help her.

She angrily pushed her chair out and stood up. She had spent so long looking through this book. It seemed right, but it was all for nothing. Her exaggerated movement caused her to knock the book onto the floor. She blushed, realizing that she had drawn attention to herself. She hated doing that. As she picked the book up to put it back on the shelf, a single page fluttered down to the ground.

"Leave it to me to damage a damn spell book." She muttered as she bent down to grab the stray page. Something about the paper grabbed her attention. It seemed to be of a heavier stock than the other pages in the book. It was a slightly different color as well, almost unnoticeable to the naked eye. She glanced at it as she was sliding it back inside with the other pages.

"Niggerimus Die" was written at the top of the page. It was an old handwritten spell. She knew from other spells she had cast that it roughly translated to "The Darkest Day" in Latin. There was no explanation as to what the spell was for or how it worked. This had to be what she was looking for. Her gut told her that it was. She folded the sheet in half and stuck it in her pocket, quickly glancing around to make sure no one saw her take it. She sent Max a quick message to say that she was on her way to his house, and she headed out. He agreed to meet her at the park at nightfall, but this couldn't wait.

The day was fairly overcast, and it seemed like a perfect time to try out the spell. She would cast it inside of the house, just to be safe. He wouldn't have to go far to find out if it worked or not. If it wasn't a success, he would probably have some minor burns, but nothing that wouldn't heal in a matter of minutes. Thank God for that rapid vampire healing. Hopefully, it wouldn't come to that.

She was surprised that he was awake when she got to his house, but he must have been excited at the possibility of getting back to a semi-normal life. Who could blame him?

"Are you ready to try this?" she asked as she walked into the basement.

"More than you can imagine babe." He said as he gave her a hug. His arms lingered around her. He was in this because of her, but she still felt like safety. Relief surged through him at the mere sight of her. He knew that she would find a way to help him.

It was weird to hug him now. He was the same Max that she had hugged before, but now he was cold and somewhat intimidating.

"You know I'm not great at spells, so please don't be mad if I don't get it right at first. I'm not even positive that I found the right thing. I have been getting better at spells lately, though. You should have seen me casting after school yesterday. My mom even came outside and pumped me up about it. That was a first." She said as she closed her eyes and tried to steady her breathing. This was the most nervous she had ever been about casting a spell. There was so much riding on this. She had studied the spell the entire way to his house, so she quickly recited it as she had done about one hundred times already.

"Aren't you going to say something?" Max asked, seeming a bit bewildered as to why Brynn was just standing there with her eyes closed.

"No." Brynn laughed as she opened her eyes. "You don't have to say the spells out loud. I'm not a witch or anything. Trust me. We only say them out loud when we are learning them for the first time. I said it out loud the whole way here. Now walk upstairs and see what happens."

Max gave her a look of extreme speculation as he headed toward the staircase. She was too nervous to watch what happened. She just closed her eyes and waited.

She took it from the scream that ensued and the subsequent string of obscenities that followed that her spell had not worked.

"I'm so sorry!" she cried out as she saw him walk back down the stairs. His face was burned and bleeding much worse than she thought that it would be. This was not a minor burn. Skin was hanging off.

"It's ok, Brynn. It will heal. Just don't start crying again." He joked as he took a seat on the edge of the bed. Thank God his parents had gone away for the weekend. There would be no way to put an innocent spin on what was happening right now. It looked like a scene straight out of a horror movie.

"I don't know how well you will heal. You haven't... fed... much, have you?"

"To be honest, I don't even really know what I am doing. I get nervous." He looked away. He felt like the worst vampire to ever have existed. Pathetic.

He was embarrassed that he had no idea what to do. The man that made him a vampire told him nothing about his new life. He managed to suck down a few small animals on his way home from the park the night before, but that was it. He didn't ask for this life, and he didn't even know how to live it properly. He felt worthless.

"Well, why don't you just have a little bit of my blood? You need to eat, or you won't heal, and I am not done trying out this spell. Plus, I learned when I was young that vamps can draw powers from those that they... feed on. I hate that term. Maybe it will help, though." Brynn realized how irrational it sounded before she was even done speaking, but he needed to eat.

"No way. I am not doing that to you. I will heal. We will just have to wait a little while. I am not poking holes in you and draining your blood in addition to everything else that has been going on."

"I know it sounds crazy, Max and I know it might be weird. I promise it will help. I wouldn't suggest it if I thought there was another way. What if it takes the rest of the day for you to heal? If we run out of sunlight, we are done trying this. We don't have any other options. Trust me, the thought of someone drinking my blood doesn't get me all giddy. It's weird for me too."

"What if I can't top once I start? It's dangerous Brynn. I might not know what I am doing or how any of this works, but I know enough to know how much I could hurt you."

"You will be able to stop yourself. When you kissed me last night, you resisted any urge you might have had. It turned out fine. You're strong and I know you won't hurt me."

"That's easy for you to say. You don't know how it felt when I kissed you. It was powerful. Almost more powerful than me."

He knew that Brynn was right. He hated it. It was a dangerous plan, but he needed to feed. He could feel himself getting weaker as he sat there rather than healing. She walked over to the bed and sat beside him. He really did feel like this was crossing a line, but what choice did he have?

She was so beautiful. If she only knew what he saw when he looked at her.

He brushed the hair away from her neck as she closed her eyes. He could see, hear, and feel the pulse in her neck. It was beating so rapidly; he knew that she was nervous. He had never felt so much desire in his life. It was like the blood was calling out to him. But it wasn't just any blood, it was hers. He felt Brynn take a deep breath when she heard his fangs come out.

The second his teeth pierced her skin; his mouth was full of blood. It flowed down his throat like hot chocolate would have when he was still a human. It seemed to hurt Brynn only for a second and then she was completely relaxed. His cold hands held her gently until he was finished. When he was done, he pierced the tip of his finger with his fang and ran some of his own blood over the bite marks. The wounds disappeared instantly. He didn't know how he knew to do that. It must have been some new vampire instinct. If he could absorb her powers, maybe she could use his. It seemed to work.

"How do you feel now?" Brynn asked him, smiling as she watched his face heal until it was perfect once again. She felt a bit woozy but was happy to see him healing.

"It was a satisfaction that I have never felt before. And at the risk of sounding disgusting, your blood tastes great."

They shared a laugh, and he tucked her hair behind her ear. Tasting her blood made him want her even more. It was distracting.

"That's good, because I want to try this one more time."

He rolled his eyes and grinned at her, fangs still out. She felt like a weirdo for thinking it, but he looked so hot in that moment. She grabbed his hand and they both stood up.

"That hurt like hell last time. Shouldn't

you sprinkle some fairy dust on me or something?"

"Fairy dust would definitely help. Unfortunately, all I can ever manage to make is fairy dirt. It, in fact, is not the same thing as dust. I found that out the hard way. Very embarrassing. No, I don't want to talk about it. Now hush and let me concentrate."

They decided to try holding hands as she cast the spell this time. She closed her eyes and began to focus harder than she ever had before. She thought about how badly she needed this spell to work. She pictured a world in which she could never again walk hand in hand with Max in the daylight. It was a dark, lonely world and it was breaking her heart just thinking about it.

She then thought about the kind of world they could have together if the spell worked. She saw them walking together down the coast of the beach, there was no one else around and the tide was rushing in and out on their feet. When they finally reached a pier, they stopped and looked at each other.

"I love you, Brynn." He said to her in the

vision. Then they shared a kiss.

She exhaled slowly and recited the spell for a second time.

"Go upstairs" she said with her eyes still closed.

He didn't say anything in response, but she could hear his footsteps as he climbed the stairs.

Silence.

"Max, say something." She barely choked out, holding back the potential tears that would be there if he was burned again.

"Brynn, open your eyes."

He was standing there in the sunlight, beaming a smile bigger than she had seen on him before.

"You did it, Brynn! Your spell worked I knew it would before I even walked upstairs. I could see what you saw as you cast it. It was like we were connected as one mind, one spirit."

All she could do was run up the stairs and

give him a hug. It was by far the biggest accomplishment of her life. If only she could share this with the others. They wouldn't think she was such a letdown if they knew that she could do this.

"Well, what do you want to do now that you can go outside safely?"

"Let's go to lunch." He said taking her hand in his.

"But you don't eat now... you don't have to go somewhere like that just for my benefit."

"I'm sure we can figure something out."

SEVEN

Brynn was excited that Max was willing to go to Zoe's Cafe. She had overheard some other fairies talking about it at home one day. It was a restaurant that was safe and accommodating for all types of mystica people. Super exciting. She never had anyone to go with before, so she was happy to have her first non-fairy friend to take with her.

It was about an hour out of the way, so she was happy to get out of the car and stretch her legs when they got there. She suggested that Max just carry her, and they could get there much faster, but he insisted on being as inconspicuous as possible. She just hoped that being gone for so long today wouldn't cause any kind of problem for her. He might not be a human anymore, but something told her this still wouldn't go over very well.

She started feeling giddy as they walked up to the restaurant. The building itself wasn't that big on the outside. It was a solid brick structure with a huge front door and no window. She assumed that was to accommodate the vampires. The sign had a blue neon light behind the "Zoe's Café" lettering.

There was a small, curved hallway after you walked in the front door leading to another door. It had to be to block out the sunlight. If you could walk straight in from outside, there were bound to be some vampires that would be burned each time someone came in. That would certainly be bad for business. There was a small wooden podium with a hostess leaning up against it when they walked in through the massive secondary front door. She smiled and showed them to a booth.

"What do you think she is?" Brynn asked Max as she glanced around at the other people in the room.

"She is definitely a wolf."

"How can you be so certain?"

"I have an awesome sense of smell now, remember?" He laughed as he jabbed her with his elbow.

"I guess I was so obsessed with the sunlight thing that I forgot about everything else. So, who are all of these other people in here then?"

"They are mostly vamps and wolves."

"How do you think the other vampires get here? Do they all have a spell cast on them or something?"

"No." Max chuckled. "There is a door in the corner that probably leads to something underground. They must come from there. You will probably be more interested in the fairy in the back, though. She didn't seem to recognize you, so she must not be part of your family."

Brynn glanced at her over her shoulder. Max was right, she had never seen this fairy before. She was relieved. She didn't want any trouble.

A teenage looking vampire came to take their order. Brynn was a bit surprised to see that they had so much normal food on the menu. The building was glamoured, so there wasn't a chance of a human coming in. It just looked like a brick wall with no entrance of any kind to any human that might be passing by. She figured that people probably assumed it was an old structure that had been bricked up for safety reasons. There was also a side menu with a raw meat section for the wolves and blood for the vampires. She wondered what other types of mystica came in that would want regular food. Was it just for fairies or were there other beings that she didn't even know about?

The growl in her stomach made her get back to the business at hand. She ordered a grilled chicken sandwich with extra pickles and fries. Max ordered something from the blood section. From what she could gather, the options were blood types.

"How do you know what kind of blood to order?"

"I don't, it was just a guess. I picked 'O' because that is either universal donor or receiver. Seems like it would be a safe bet. Hopefully, it won't be something disgusting. If such a concept exists for a vampire. I'm guessing it is kind of like ordering wine. We will see."

They continued to play their supernatural guessing game while they waited for their food to arrive. There were only a few people whose smell Max could not identify. She was going to have to do some research on them when she got home. It was exciting to think about what else could be out there with them. They learned about mystica, but she always felt like they weren't being told everything. It wasn't a bit hard to concentrate with her stomach growling so loudly, though. Luckily, it wasn't long before their food arrived.

There wasn't anything fancy about the dishes their meals came on. She was hoping Max's beverage would come in a fancy wine glass or chalice, but it arrived in a plain drinking glass. It was slightly disappointing, but that thought quickly left her head once she tasted her sandwich.

"Did they glamour this thing to taste so good?" she asked out loud with a mouthful of food and a bit of a moan.

Max said nothing but offered her a grin as he sipped on his drink. She had no idea how cute she was to him right now.

Brynn engulfed half of her sandwich in the blink of an eye. She hadn't noticed just how hungry she was until she began to taste her food. Max was right – he *had* drained her.

"So, your spell casting has gotten much better all of a sudden. What do you think the reason is?"

"I don't know. I am pretty happy about it, though. It kinda sucks messing up all of the time." She kept trying to swallow her bites quickly so she wouldn't be talking with a mouthful of food. The sandwich was too good to put down.

"How do you do it?"

"What? Casting?"

"Yeah."

"Different ways. Sometimes there are phrases that I have to recite. Some spells work by visualizing and manifesting."

"Have you gotten better at all of it or just one of the methods?"

"Both. One way doesn't seem more successful than the other. Why are you so curious about it?"

"I don't know. I'm curious about all of it, actually. I never thought that any of this stuff existed. Now I'm living it and I want to learn all that I can." He smiled as he took another sip of his drink.

"How is your beverage?" She asked Max with another mouthful of food, but Max didn't respond. He just sat there motionless, as if he had seen a ghost.

Yikes. She should probably mind her manners if she wanted to keep her new boyfriend.

"Max?" He didn't even flinch. His eyes were fixed on something behind her.

"Dude. You are starting to freak me out. What's wrong with you?"

EIGHT

"Hello, Brynn."

The voice coming from behind startled her. She quickly swallowed her food before starting to turn around. The man behind the voice had beautiful golden curls covering the sides of his pale face. His eyes were a stunning mix of green and gold in a brilliant starburst pattern.

"I'm glad to find you doing so well, Max. I see that someone has already figured out your daylight conundrum. I didn't notice you downstairs, so I am assuming that you came from the outside. Is that right? Well done, filia." He winked at Brynn.

"Max, do you know this guy? What's going on?" Brynn asked, feeling more confused now than she was when she found out Fiona was trying to help her. Why did this kind of thing keep happening to her?

"My sweet Brynn, I think that you know who I am." As if on cue, his wings came out with his last word. They were beautiful. They were huge and white, just like hers.

"Your wings..." she trailed off, wonder in her eyes. She had never seen another person with angel wings. How was this possible?

"This is the man who turned me into a vampire, Brynn." Max finally spoke, but in such a whisper she could barely hear him.

"I am much more than your maker, Maximillian. I must apologize, I suppose I never did properly introduce myself to you. My name is..."

"Vincent. Your name is Vincent, isn't it?" Brynn whispered as a tear fell from her eye. She couldn't believe it was really him.

"What the hell is going on Brynn?" Max asked, almost shouting. She could feel the anger ready to pour out of him. "Who the hell is this guy? How do you know him? Is he friends with Fiona or something? Do you know him too?"

"I am her father, Max. She has been kept away from me since she was merely a toddler. When Fiona spoke to me about Brynn and a mortal boy, I knew I had to help her. This was my chance to be there for her in a way that no one else would be so willing."

"That doesn't even make sense, man. How can you be Brynn's father if you are a vampire? And help her? This seems like a far cry from help." Max demanded.

"Supernatural lines do not always create immunity from one another. A fairy, such as I, can be turned into a vampire just as easily as a human can. A fairy can just as easily become a wolf. I was turned into a vampire after Fiona was born. The others would not accept me any longer, so I was forced to withdraw from the life I knew and loved. I wanted my family to come with me, but Shyan would have nothing to do with it. I had no choice but to leave and watch my family grow from a distance. I reached out to Fiona a few years ago and we have kept our relationship a secret from everyone. They would send her away if they knew she was speaking with me."

Brynn just sat at the table silently crying. Her entire world had just been set in a tailspin. She was furious at Fiona for keeping this secret and their father all to herself. She was angry at her mother for choosing to keep them away from him. And why Fiona anyway? Why was she the only one who got to have this secret family connection? So far, the only thing she *wasn't* mad about was him turning Max into a vampire. None of this made any sense.

"Why don't we go somewhere a little more private?" Vincent suggested, seeing how flustered Brynn was getting, and they both got up from their seats and followed him to the door leading underground. They had far too many questions to protest. Both of them needed answers.

It was cold and dark underneath the restaurant. There were different paths jetting off in various directions. It was as if there were passageways to anywhere a vampire would need to go. This was a good thing to keep in mind for Max if and when the sunlight spell stopped working. As it stood, neither of them knew how long it might hold up.

Vincent seemed to know where he was going. How long had it all been down here she wondered. He definitely seemed to know the underground system well. Being a vampire for thirteen years, she was sure he knew a lot of things vital to staying alive. Those were all tips that she hoped he planned to share with Max. She didn't know a great deal about vampires, but it was always said that makers had a close relationship with their progenies. So far, that wasn't the case at all.

They stopped walking when they came to a door. "Aliger" was written on the front in gold script. It was her last name. She knew that they had arrived at her father's house. Vincent slipped an ornate skeleton key into the lock, and they followed him inside.

It was exactly what she expected a

vampire's house to look like. It was very dark with a small bed in the corner draped in black satin bedding. On the other side of the room was a black leather couch and recliner. There appeared to be an upper level, but the door leading upstairs was closed. She assumed that the majority of his time was spent downstairs where there were no windows. It was still daylight outside, so she understood why he didn't invite them upstairs. They each took a seat on the couch as Vincent lit a few candles.

"Why haven't you helped Max adjust to his new life? You just turned him and left him. I thought that makers were close with their progenies." Vincent looked surprised at Brynn's sudden urge to speak up. The question also seemed to catch him off guard. He was probably expecting a barrage of questions about her personal life, but right now she was more concerned for Max.

"You are right, and I have every intention of having that relationship with Max. I needed to wait until the time was right. I was waiting for a time like this. I knew if Max spent time with me, he would know that you and I were connected. That wouldn't be safe for you.

Plus, I wanted you to find all of this out from me, not someone else."

The candles flickered behind them. Max was still sitting silently, trying to take everything in. His anger was slowly fading, but it was just met with more confusion.

"It is especially important, Brynn, for you to keep all of this a secret. If you are to have any type of normal life, the others can never know that you are seeing me. They will cast you out in the blink of an eye and your mother will be too afraid to speak up on your behalf. It is a risk to even speak of it with Fiona. She was lucky to not get caught approaching me with your predicament. That goes for Max as well. Even though he is no longer in danger for knowing about what you are, they will still send you away for having a relationship with him. They do not trust vampires."

"Maybe I don't want a normal life. I hate it at home. I suck at spell casting, and everyone treats me like an outsider. Why would I want to stay there if I had a chance to live a different life? It's a shitty life."

"Because different is not always better, Brynn. You have the protection of the other fairies there. You would be on your own without them and trust me, there are a lot of people who would kill a fairy just for getting in their way. The only reason I have survived this long is because I am also a vampire. I can't make you do anything, especially after so many years of absence. I'm just asking you to think about it." He ran his fingers though his hair, clearly overwhelmed.

"Why Fiona?" she asked meagerly. Her veracity was starting to fade.

"What do you mean?"

"I mean, why her and not me? Do you know what a punch to the gut it is to find out she has gotten to know you? I'm left out of everything. She treats me like shit. Everyone ignores me at home. My casting is inconsistent at very best. Fiona gets it all. Why her?"

"Brynn, I am sorry for what life has been for you. I mean it when I say that it hurts me to know. I begged to not be separated from you girls. As for why her, it was all about opportunity. H happened to be somewhere alone. I saw her and decided to approach. It wasn't safe for me to find you yet."

Brynn brushed her long brown hair out of her face and began wrapping the blue part around one of her fingers. Twirling her hair was a nervous habit she had had since she was a small child. Most of the time she didn't even realize she was doing it.

"Ok, I will think about it then. I'm not making any promises, though. Why do they hate vampires so much that they would cast you out anyway?"

"It is because of fear. Vampires once threatened the very existence of fairies. It was thought that if you consumed the blood of the fae, you could absorb their powers. There was a rampage fueled by horrible bloodlust. It was so bad. It could have wiped everyone out."

"Is that true? Is our blood that powerful?"

"Why don't you ask Max? He did taste your blood, didn't he?"

She didn't even ask how he knew about that. Blood rushed to her cheeks, and she knew that there was no concealing her embarrassment. She turned to Max who seemed surprised to be questioned. Neither of them tried to deny that it happened.

"I don't feel like I have any type of new power. I wouldn't really know how to find out anyway." Max said with a frown. "It was powerful, though and I healed quickly after. I just figured that would happen with any blood. I had nothing to compare it too."

She smiled at Max and was surprised about how at ease she felt sitting in the home of a man she knew nothing about. And in a home where she was alone with vampires at that. Something about Vincent seemed genuine. She didn't think that he was lying to her about anything. So far Fiona had been safe, and she had spent time with him. Besides, he turned Max for her. Even if the others did find out about them, now she knew that they would just cast her out rather than trying to eradicate either of them. As crazy as it all was, it was a relief.

"You should be getting back before they suspect something. You can get out from upstairs. I'm sure you will understand if I don't show you out. While I still possess my fairy powers, I choose not to use them on myself. It is safer for me that way. If you need me for anything Brynn, just have Max summon me. As for you Maximillian, meet me here tonight to begin your vampire 101 lessons. We will get this relationship on the right track. I'm sorry it has taken this long." He chuckled as they headed upstairs.

NINE

The drive and subsequent walk home was uneventful for both of them. When Brynn's mom asked her where she had been all day, she told her that she had lunch with a friend from school.

"Be careful, Brynn." Her mom didn't seem to like it, but it wasn't a lie, and it was certainly better than the full truth. Despite what her father had told her, she really wanted to talk with Fiona. She had so many questions that only her sister could answer. She planned to try to sneak into her room after dinner.

Once she got to the kitchen, though, Fiona's spot at the table was empty. It was the first time she had not been with the family for dinner since she accidentally cast a sneezing spell on herself five years ago. Though it was funny, no one wanted to eat sneezed on food. Brynn tried to act like nothing was wrong and sat through the meal with everyone else. No one mentioned it, and considering her strained relationship with her sister, asking at the table would have raised suspicion.

Her mom excused herself early saying she didn't feel well. Brynn wanted to run after her but managed to play it cool. She needed to wait. Once everyone was finished eating and the tablet had been cleared, she went to her mother's room.

"Mom, have you seen Fiona?"

Her mother was just sitting on the side of her pastel-colored bed, almost stoic. It was unlike her to be a recluse, especially so close to dinner time.

"Fiona is gone." Was her simple response as she still sat there emotionless.

"What do you mean she is gone? Where did she go?" Panic rushed over Brynn like a wave. She could feel her pulse racing and her palms became clammy.

"You know exactly what I mean, Brynn. Shyan turned to look at her daughter. "And if you aren't careful, you will be gone as well. Don't think I don't know what you have been up to. I can smell the vampire on you. You are just lucky that nobody around here pays much attention to you, or they would smell you too. I mean really, Brynn. How could you girls be so stupid?"

"So, what then, are you just going to turn your back on Fiona like you did our father?"

"Young lady you are out of line. That is a story that you know nothing about. What you think you know is wrong. You need to go to your room and stay there before someone overhears you."

That was no problem. She was happy to go to her room. How could her mother just let them send Fiona, her own daughter, away? Vincent had been right on the money. There was no way that she was going to sit around and wait for the elders to come for her too. She sent Max a quick SOS text and packed her bags. This was it.

She slithered out of her window and made her way to the crack in the fence that she had come to rely on. She tossed her bags over the fence and squeezed her way out. Adrenaline was coursing through her. This would be the riskiest move she had even made in her life. There was no turning back now. She hurriedly made her way to the park.

Max was sitting in the gazebo when she got there. Thank God for that vampire speed. He smiled sympathetically at Brynn when he saw her. He felt bad that so much in her life was going wrong. Sure, he had been turned into a vampire, but that wasn't all bad. He would be young and powerful forever. He could protect her. But she tried so hard and constantly got the short end of the stick. She deserved more.

She tried to force a smile as she made her way to him. She gave him a hug and thanked him for meeting her.

"I was on my here before I even received your text. I could just sense what you needed me to do. Vincent said it was because I had consumed your blood. It is fascinating, like I can feel some of what you are feeling. It was just like when I could see the spell you were casting that day."

"I can't go back there, Max." Brynn sobbed at the thought of everything falling apart. She had been holding it together on her way to the park, but it finally hit her. Her mother with no backbone just letting Fiona be cast out... what a coward. Who treats their children like that?

"I know you can't. I am sorry about your sister. You both should be able to count on your mom. I know it's gotta hurt babe. Come with me to your father's house. He is expecting you."

Brynn didn't protest. She didn't know where else to go and she did think that she would be safe there. Who knows how long she would be safe in her own house now. It was dark outside, so they didn't have to take any underground passage. She tried to memorize the way that they were taking to get there so she would be able to come and go on her own.

The walk was long, and she began to think about the recent events of her life. It seemed like no matter what she did, she was always disappointing someone. Her spells were usually failures, she couldn't make fairy dust, she inadvertently had her boyfriend turned into a vampire and now she was leaving her mother behind. Her mother who apparently didn't give a shit about anybody except herself. It still felt wrong, though.

"Don't get yourself down, Brynn. You are beautiful and more powerful than you realize. You made me able to walk in the sun! Do you even realize how amazing that is? You even figured it out on your own. No one gave you the spell to try. You are so special. And I'm sorry, I'm not trying to pry on your emotions. I can't help but feel them and I don't know how to stop it. You don't deserve to be feeling so miserable."

"It's ok. I appreciate your kind words more

than you know. Well, I suppose you do know. Are we almost there?" She took his hand in hers, enjoying the comfort that it brought.

"We are very close to Vincent's house."

He was right. It had been less than five minutes when they finally arrived at her father's house. This was the first time that she had a chance to really look at it closely. She had been in a hurry when she left earlier in the day. It was a beautiful brick home. There was a large wooden porch that wrapped around the sides adorned with swings and tables. The two front windows were covered in satin curtains. It looked like a normal, human household.

They walked inside and Brynn was surprised to be greeted by her sister.

"Brynn, oh my God! What are you doing here? Did anyone see you leave?" Fiona cried out as she hugged her sister. This was the first time that Brynn had ever felt like Fiona was happy to see her. In fact, this might be the first time they willingly hugged each other.

"I don't think anyone noticed, but I don't think they will be looking for me anyway. Mom was pretty clear that my days were numbered, so I decided to leave on my own terms. What happened to you?"

"When I got home today, the elders were in my room. They told me that I reeked of vampire stink, and they would not let a traitor remain in their house. I barely had time to pack a bag before they made me leave. Mom just stood there and watched. She didn't even say a damn word to me." Fiona was so angry; she didn't know whether she wanted to cry or punch something. "What about you? What happened? Did anyone tell you what happened to me?"

"When I went down for dinner, I noticed that you were missing. Afterwards I went upstairs to mom's room and asked where you were. She told me that I smelled like a vampire and that I was lucky that nobody in the house paid attention to me. I couldn't stay there knowing she so easily turned her back on you. If she could do that to her favorite daughter, who knows what she would do to me."

"Well, I am glad that you are here with me. I am sorry for taking you for granted all this time. Ugh, I have been such a total bitch to you. I think deep down I resented you for how much you reminded me of dad. When we were little, I found a bunch of pictures of him in mom's room. I memorized his face and every time I looked at you, I saw him. I promise to make everything up to you somehow."

They sat on the couch with each other for a few minutes before Vincent came in.

"It is good to see you again so soon, Brynn. I'm sorry it had to be on such unfortunate circumstances. You can make yourself at home. There is plenty of room for both you and Fiona. As you can guess, I don't have any food in the house. You will have to go grocery shopping. There is money on the table for whatever you need. The only thing I ask while you are here is that you girls stay in school. It is important to pretend that everything is normal for right now. I will be asleep while you should be there, and I trust you two to respect my wishes. That goes for you as well Max. You will be able to sleep for a few hours before dawn and again when you get home from school. Brynn can keep the sunlight spell cast on you, so you should be safe."

Something about Vincent seemed so happy at this moment. He had given Brynn a lecture on staying with the other fairies as long as she could this morning, but she suspected that he was pleased to have his children there with him.

They all agreed to his wishes. They were lucky enough to have a place to stay and they weren't willing to jeopardize it. There were only a few weeks of the school year left anyway. It would be awkward being around the other fairies, but Brynn doubted that any of them would even speak to her or her sister. As long as the three of them stuck together, they would be okay.

Fiona showed Brynn to her new room. It was eerily similar to her old room. The same four post bed frame with a white canopy, only now her comforter was purple as were her curtains. She loved it. She sat her bag down on the bed and began to unpack her things. Max would be out with her father for a few more hours. She took a shower and slipped into bed.

It was strange that the house was furnished with beds and such things. Brynn knew her father never used them. It was almost as if he had been hoping for the chance to have her and Fiona there with him one day. She closed her eyes and cast a quick spell on herself. It should make her calm and bring ease. Her nerves were fried at this point. It seemed to work. Her eyelids became heavy, and she quickly began to fall asleep. Usually, she saw spells when she closed her eyes, but now she only saw darkness.

TEN

A knock at the door woke Brynn from the most restful sleep that she had had in months. Her spell definitely worked. Another success in the books. She imagined that Fiona had probably done the same thing after seeing how refreshed she looked when she entered the bedroom.

"Are you ready for today?" Fiona asked as

she was brushing her shimmery hair.

"As ready as I can be, I guess. It will be weird seeing the rest of them. I am sure they know all about our new associations by now. Just stick with me today. I know it will be strange for you since you are normally glued to their sides. My friends won't mind you being with us."

"Thanks." Fiona said with a forced smile. She was appreciative of Brynn's kindness, but she was right. She wouldn't know how to act at that school without being around her friends. She always thought the notion of blending into society was dumb. Now she was going to have to try to do just that. She hoped that she could succeed. There was no way that she would be able to do as good a job as Brynn had done over the years.

Brynn truly did feel sorry for her little sister. It wasn't going to be much different for her personally. The other fairies already treated her like an outcast. Fiona was going to be completely out of place, though. Max and Brynn wouldn't treat her any different than their other friends and she hoped that Fiona knew that. Maybe it would at least make things somewhat easier.

They had to leave a little earlier than usual since they were living farther away from school now. She went into the basement and cast the sunshine spell on Max again before they left. She didn't know how long the spell would last, so she didn't want to chance him going outside without it. It must have worked because he was fine when he went upstairs.

The walk to school was pretty quiet. Brynn knew that Fiona was nervous. When they were getting ready for school this morning, she noticed that the polish on her usually perfectly manicured nails was chipped away, and her makeup was a bit messy. Brynn didn't think talking would take her mind off things, though. Instead, she spent most of her time trying to remember which way she was going. It was a good thing that Fiona and Max were with her because she probably wouldn't remember how to get home. She had never been good with directions anyway.

There were only a few homes past her father's. The rest of the space was occupied by small businesses. There were a couple of barber shops, consignment stores, family restaurants and gas stations. There were well manicured lawns along the way. It was an enjoyable time of year to be outside. The weather was humid and incredibly hot today, but she overlooked all of that to be able to enjoy the smell of the wildflowers in bloom.

She kept sneaking glances at Fiona the entire way there. She was nervously picking the glittery polish off of her fingernails. Max seemed preoccupied. He was quiet and oblivious to anything going on. She wanted to reach out and grab Fiona's hand but decided not to. She felt bad for her, but she was still unsure of how to act. Two days ago, they were enemies. This newfound friendship was still a bit awkward for Brynn. She thought about how she interacted with her other friends. What would she do if it were one of them instead of her sister? She didn't have much time to ponder the thought before she saw their school up ahead in the distance.

The big stone sign displaying the words "Mitchell Browning High School" in thick black font was peeking through the usual morning fog. It was set in the middle of a sea of bright green Bermuda grass so brilliant it looked like it had been painted. There were groups of people standing around outside, but no fairies as far as she could see.

Fiona grasped Brynn's hand and as if they had done it hundreds of times before and gave her a squeeze.

"At least we can't cast any negative spells on each other. They can't really hurt you today. Well, just your feelings I guess." Brynn said to her, trying to be reassuring.

She was being truthful. She figured that if they were able to cast anything other than a healing spell on each other it would be dangerous for them. God must have kept that in mind when the fairies were cast down so long ago. After all, they were too impure and mischievous for heaven. The thought of sabotage had to have come up at some point. She had always thought the notion was silly, but not today. It would definitely keep the chaos at bay.

They said their goodbyes as Fiona headed to her homeroom class which was separate from Brynn and Max's. Fiona was a year younger than the two of them, so she would be on her own during her classes. She would be joined, unfortunately, by a few other fairies. Brynn would have her own share of fairy adversaries in her day too, but she was used to them ignoring her. Plus, she had Max to encourage her when she needed it.

"She will be fine, babe. You can stop worrying." Max said as he rubbed Brynn's back.

"I keep forgetting you have a direct line to my emotions. I know she'll be okay. She's just not used to being a loner. I doubt that she will be able to handle it as well as me." Brynn said with a sigh as they took their seats in homeroom.

She sat in the same seat she had been in since the beginning of the semester. Max had been occupying the seat next to hers since he had arrived. The morning announcements were a blur. She spoke up during roll call, but that was about it. The bell rang and everyone got up to head to their first class of the day.

"I'll see you in third period. Just focus on what's going on in class. Time will pass more quickly that way than if you just sit and think about your sister." Max kissed her on the forehead and headed off in the opposite direction. Brynn knew that he was right, but it was easier said than done.

She did her best to focus on schoolwork and like Max had promised, the day went by pretty quickly. That was more than could be said for Fiona, however. She was almost in tears by the time Brynn saw her in the hall.

"Are you okay?" Brynn asked as she approached her.

"Yeah, I'm just ready to go home. Those guys are such jerks. I am sorry I ever acted like that to you. How did you not punch me in the face or something?" Fiona sighed as she laid her head on Brynn's shoulder. She smirked at the question.

"I know you are. It's in the past, though. We are lucky enough to get a fresh start. What did they say to you?"

"Nothing really. Addison called me a traitor and Shania kept throwing paper at me. I think there may have been a few spitballs. Gross. It just hurts knowing that they were my friends yesterday and they so quickly turned their backs on me without even knowing the truth of the situation. No one even asked me for my side of the story. They are just so ignorant. I hate that I was like that. Ugh! Why was I like that?" She tossed her head back in what appeared to be a mixture of disgust and exasperation. Sometimes it was tough to look at yourself in the mirror.

"I'm sure they think that they *do* know the truth and the truth hurts when you're living a lie. They would feel differently if they knew everything. You can't hold this against them. I swear everyone there is brainwashed. I'm glad we see the truth now. I promise that you will get through this. Why don't you go in the bathroom and cast a courage spell or something? It will probably help."

Fiona took her sister's advice and retreated to the bathroom to cast the spell. Once they parted, Brynn saw one of the fairy boys ahead of her.

"Drake!" she yelled at him and tried to catch up. She needed to say something to defend her sister.

"Oh, hey Brynn. What's up?" She was startled by his casual response.

"Aren't you going to call me a traitor or something?"

"Just because I haven't been banished from our family doesn't mean that I don't know there is more to the story. Here, read this when you aren't near any of the other fairies and *please* don't let them know I gave this to you." He discreetly slipped a folded-up piece of paper into her hand and lost her in the crowd of other students.

Drake was one of the few fairies that didn't treat her badly. She never knew why, but she appreciated it. She fought the urge to open up the paper and see what it said. The only place she could be alone and sure that no one else would see it was at her home.

Home. It felt so strange to call it that. Last week it was a place that she didn't even know existed, now it was the place that she lived with her sister and long-lost father. And despite all of the anger that she felt, she wished that her mother was there with them. She didn't mention the note to Max when she saw him in third period. In fact, she left Drake out of the conversation entirely. She instead told him only about Fiona and the courage spell.

"That must be what you seem so apprehensive about." He said so casually, as if it were normal to know what she was feeling. She supposed it *was* normal for him at this point. Would it ever be normal for her? Some feelings and thoughts she would be horrified for him to know about.

She was glad that he had just assumed that was what her mind was focused on rather than asking her. She would have had to tell him then. She was sure that she would clue him in, but she wanted to know what the note said before she made that decision. She changed the subject to the homework assignments that she had been given so far and tried to keep their conversations centered around school issues for the rest of the day.

She didn't see Fiona again until school was over with. Brynn was waiting out front by the school sign when she saw her walk outside. They waited there for Max and the three of them began to walk home.

"I forgot to ask you something Max." Brynn began. "What did you tell your mom about where you were staying if you are going to be spending so much time with my dad? I assume you will be living there as well."

"It was convenient timing, actually. She and my stepdad have been fighting a lot lately and it has been really tense there. So, I told her yesterday that I didn't want to deal with it anymore. I am eighteen and legally free to live wherever I choose. So, I packed my bags and told her I would call her when I felt like the time was right. She has been so caught up in her own drama that she barely seemed to care. Honestly, it is probably easier on her if I'm not there."

"That seems really easy. She just let you go?" Fiona chimed in.

"Well, I may have used my persuasive vampire charms a bit as well. You guys aren't the only ones who can do that I have learned. I told Vincent what I was planning to do, so he gave me a quick lesson in charm school. It worked pretty well."

The three of them laughed as they made

their way down the sidewalk. They were all so relieved to be out of school for the day that they were in pretty high spirits, even Fiona.

"So, Max, what new things have you noticed about yourself since becoming a vampire?" Fiona asked in a tone that suggested that she was a little nervous to ask.

"Quite a bit. I guess I could break it down into pros and cons.

Pros: heightened senses, super-fast speed, super strong, cool new eyes, new family.

Cons: the sun is still a little uncomfortable to be in even with the spell, I can hear people's pulses, I miss feeling warm, I'll never enjoy a good cheeseburger again."

"Ooh, the cheeseburger thing got me. That sucks dude. I'm sorry." She genuinely sounded apologetic.

Truth be told, she did feel bad now. Him becoming a vampire was her call. Vincent may have facilitated it, but she was the mastermind. Now that she knew him, she may have made a different decision.

"I never said the cons outweigh the pros. Yeah, there are a lot of things that I miss. There is a silver lining, though. Don't beat yourself up, Fiona." He gave her a smile. It was the truth. It wasn't all bad. Complicated, yes, but not a complete disaster.

The rest of the walk was pretty quiet aside from a bit of humming and the sound of their footsteps. Brynn's stomach began to growl, and she suddenly remembered that there was no food in the house that they were returning to.

"Do you guys' mind stopping at the grocery store on the corner? I won't survive if we don't pick up some food." She asked the others.

"I am so glad that you remembered!" Fiona replied. "Do you have that money dad left?"

Brynn nodded her head and they walked into the grocery store. Max had no requests, of course. So, the girls picked out their favorite foods and loaded up the cart. Neither of them really knew how to cook, so they were sure to grab things that were easy to make.

"Unlike you pioneer women," Max chuckled, "I do know how to cook. So just let me know if you want me to make you something. It won't bother me. Food doesn't disgust me; it just doesn't interest me."

They both giggled, a bit embarrassed by his acknowledgement of their lack of modern skills. The gesture very much was appreciated, though. You could only eat so many pizza pockets and frozen meals.

"We will take you up on that this weekend. I know you have to sleep as soon as we get home today. Brynn said as she slid her hand into Max's on their way out of the grocery store.

"I don't know how I am going to do that. I am wide awake. How am I just supposed to turn my brain off until dark?"

"One of us can cast a spell on you to help you fall asleep." Fiona said while falling a few steps behind them.

"That's a good idea. Being friends with fairies is certainly coming in handy for me." Max joked as the three of them shared in idle chit chat on what was left of the walk home.

"Also, let's drive to school tomorrow guys. Now that we have gotten a feel for where things are, I think we will be good. This is a longer walk than I expected." Fiona said sounding exhausted.

"That's a great idea. Walking sucks when you have the speed of a vampire but aren't using it."

Brynn decided to let Fiona cast the spell on Max when they got home. It would give her a chance to go to her room and read the note that Drake gave her. They left the groceries on the kitchen table and agreed to meet back there in ten minutes. That would give Fiona enough time to cast her spell.

Brynn locked the door behind her when she entered her room. She pulled the folded up note out of the front pocket of her jeans, sat down on her bed, and started to read.

"Brynn, the nature of this note is serious, and I hope that you heed this warning. Your mother is in danger by staying here at the compound. With your sister gone and rumors circulating that your father is a vampire, the elders won't stand for her presence. They are

beginning to think that her indifference is nothing more than a farce. The discontent within the family is growing. I know that no one else is going to reach out to you, so I am forced to write you this letter. I love Fiona too much to see anything bad happen to her. I ask that you keep our communication as much of a secret as you can. If the elders find out that I know any of their secrets, it is certain that I will be in danger as well. Please, get your mother to safety. Tell Fiona that I am sorry... and that I love her. I love her so very much."

Brynn's heart sank deep into her stomach. She had been furious at her mother for turning her back on them, but now that had all been replaced with fear. How could they possibly get her to leave? If she hadn't gone after her children on her own, what else could they try? She didn't want to get Drake in trouble, but she had to tell the others. She was baffled by the part about Fiona, though. From what she could tell, they barely even spoke to each other at home. What was this? Some sort of secret relationship?

She heard Fiona's footsteps in the hall, so she got up and unlocked her door.

"Can I come in?" she heard Fiona ask as she knocked on her door.

"Of course, you can come in. Did the spell work?"

"Yep, he was asleep before I even left his room. I decided to come looking for you when you weren't back in the kitchen. What have you been doing this whole time? Just sitting here on your bed? Are you feeling alright?"

"No, I was reading something. I would explain it to you, but it is probably just better for you to read it for yourself." She handed the note to Fiona as she took a seat on the bed. She didn't know what the situation between Fiona and Drake was exactly, but there was clearly something there. It would mean more for her to read it herself.

Brynn sat there trying to read the expression on Fiona's face. As she put the letter down, a tear fell from her eye.

"I miss him so much. I didn't even get a chance to say goodbye to him." Fiona began to sob into her hands.

"I didn't even know that you two were

close." Brynn was so confused. She seemed to stay confused these days.

"We have been going out for over a year. We have kept it a secret from literally everyone. We thought that it would just complicate things for people to know. Plus, I didn't want him to be in danger if they found out that I had been sneaking away to see dad. It was dangerous enough for me, I couldn't ask him to risk his life too. You can understand that. I know how worried must have been about Max."

"Does he know the truth about dad?"

"Yes, I finally told him. I needed him to understand why we needed to keep things a secret. You can trust him, Brynn. If he says mom is in danger, then she most certainly is. We have to get her out of there. I know she left us hanging, but she's still our mom."

Brynn sighed, rubbing her brow lightly. Fiona was right. They had to do something before it was too late. It would take more than just the two of them, though.

They sat there on the bed trying to come up with ideas. Once Max and Vincent were finally awake, they hoped to come up with a better formulated plan. They decided to go downstairs and put away the groceries as they continued to plot.

"We may as well eat dinner." Fiona said, realizing that they hadn't eaten yet as her stomach began to growl in protest. "We will be pretty useless if we are starving."

"Let's just make the frozen pizza. It is the easiest thing that we got from the store."

They made the pizza and ate in silence. It wasn't the best dinner in the world. Despite cooking it at the right temperature for exactly the right amount of time, it was still burnt. Fiona didn't seem to mind, but Brynn finically picked the charred pepperoni off one by one, leaving only the crust and cheese to eat.

"Too bad there isn't a spell to cast to make this taste better." Brynn joked and Fiona laughed along with her. They were both looking forward to Max cooking for them this weekend.

They were both staring out of the window, waiting for the sun to set. As soon as it was below the horizon, Vincent would be awake. It was like some weird instinct that vampires had. Even after brainstorming for the rest of the afternoon, neither of them had come up with a good plan on how to get their mother to leave the fairy compound. They were each secretly trying not to let panic set in. Vincent would surely have a plan.

ELEVEN

So, we need a plan to rescue your mother, do we?" Vincent's voice and statement surprised the girls, who had fallen asleep in the living room while waiting for their father and Max to wake up. They both jolted awake at the sound.

"How do you know that already? We

haven't told you anything yet." Brynn asked, rubbing her eyes.

Just because a vampire is sleeping, my dear, does not mean that he or she cannot hear you. Our hearing has evolved far beyond what you have been taught at the compound. I also take it that you haven't come up with a solid plan yet, is that correct?"

Brynn and Fiona nodded their heads, visibly disappointed in their failure. Max walked over to Brynn and put his arm around her. He didn't have to say anything, she knew that he could sense the worry and fear that she was currently feeling. She wondered if her emotional roller coaster was making him nauseous yet.

"Let's begin our plan then, now that we are all awake. Max and I obviously cannot go near the compound. Those vampire wards that they have up would fry us in an instant. What about your friend... Drake, is it? Would he be of any help to us or is his allegiance to the family too strong?"

Fiona sat there for a moment in a quick inner debate. "I think he would help us. He already took a substantial risk writing that note. Truthfully, I think his loyalty might be with me."

"That would be very helpful. The next obstacle that we are faced with is the fact that we will not be able to lie, except for Max. Even being part vampire now, I am still bound by the fairy rules. If we have to tell any untruths, it will be up to Max to handle that."

Max agreed that it would be no problem for him to lie. Now that he was a vampire, he was ready to have a chance to be ruthless. He wanted to see what he was made of. Hopefully, he wouldn't be disappointed in himself.

"I will be honest with you girls. I have been trying for many years to find a way to get your mother out of there. I do still love her, even if she did turn her back on me. There has never been another woman in my life. There never will be. I have come up with so many scenarios over the years. Now that you two are with me. I think I have one that just might work."

It was hard for Brynn and Fiona not to

smile at his admission. They were both filled with hope and a sense of family unity. It was something that Brynn was definitely not used to feeling. Her heart felt warm and oddly at ease. It was something that she always yearned for... a loving, united family.

"If Max takes Fiona's phone and can get a message to Drake saying that she is in trouble, Drake will think that it is Fiona asking for help. He will have no reason to think about Max, nor will he have any idea that it is a lie. If Drake can get that message to Shyan, I am hoping that she will feel compelled to leave the compound. When she gets here, she will see that there is no emergency. So, our challenge at that point will be to keep her here. If only I knew what was making her feel forced to stay there, despite the absence of her family. The Seelie Court has caused her to experience so much loss; Madeleine, me and you two girls. Yet still, she shows unwavering loyalty to them."

Nobody had any idea about what her reason for staying could be. That knowledge would definitely have given them a leg up, but they would just have to move on. Anything that they came up with would just be mere speculation. There was too big of a chance that it could send them in the wrong direction. There would be no room for mistakes.

"So, what should the emergency be?" Max asked.

"I would have to be pretty close to death for her to leave, I think." Fiona said, sounding sad at the measures it may take for her mother to show that she cared for her.

"What about a vampire attack?" Brynn asked, cringing at the words. Even thinking about exploiting the vicious vampire stereotype made her a bit uncomfortable.

"I think that might be a little too severe. She might assume that it would be too late for her to do anything." Vincent brought up a good point. Now she was a little embarrassed that she suggested such a thing. No one seemed to take offence, though.

"What if Max says that I got hit by a car on my way home from school? That I am pretty banged up and I desperately need her. I need blood, but I am too scared to go to a human hospital because of what I am. I also

138

want to make sure we ask Drake not to come. I don't want him in trouble because of me."

"That is a fantastic idea, Fiona! What do you think Vincent?" Max asked excitedly.

"I think that for someone who cannot lie herself, she can dream up quite the story. I agree. Let's do it."

"Are you sure that you don't want Drake to come with her, Fiona? We don't know if there will be another chance to get him out."

"Yes. I can't force that decision upon him. Plus, it might be helpful to keep an ally on the inside for right now." It's not what she really wanted, but she couldn't be selfish. She didn't want Drake to leave everything behind only to end up resenting her for it.

Fiona retrieved her phone from her backpack and handed it to Max. He immediately began texting.

"Drake, I need your help. I need my mom. Please. I got hit by a car on my way home from school. My father says I need blood. Mom is the only one who can give it to me. I can't go to a human hospital... they will know that I am

different. Mom will know the address. She needs to hurry. Please don't risk your safety coming with her. I will be okay once I get the blood. Just make sure that she gets here." Max read the message out loud as he typed it. Everyone agreed that it sounded good, and he hit the send button.

"Right away. Just hold on Fi." Drake texted back almost immediately.

Everyone breathed a sigh of relief. Their plan had depended on a fairy that may or may not be willing to help them. It was up to Shyan now. No one knew quite what to expect. Would she come right away? Brynn assumed her mother knew the address because of the letter that she had found stashed away in the dresser drawer. Surely her mother would have never taken the risk to come here before.

They all sat around for hours looking at each other, not saying a word. Brynn and Fiona were both visibly fighting drowsiness and disappointment. What if she didn't come?

"Why don't you two get some sleep?" Max asked in a voice that suggested that he felt sorry for them.

"No, it's nothing a spell can't fix." Brynn replied as she and Fiona closed their eyes in unison.

Whatever spell they were casting appeared to help. Max could see the color returning to their faces before they even opened their eyes.

"It must be nice being able to cast a spell to fix almost anything." Max said with envy. The girls just giggled.

"Your mother is almost here." Vincent said suddenly, causing everyone's laughter to cease immediately.

"How do you know that?"

"I could never forget your mother's scent, Brynn. It is all that I can smell right now. I suggest you all prepare yourselves. Just because she is here does not mean that she will stay or cooperate once she sees that Fiona is not in danger. Fiona, I suggest that you go to your room. Perhaps if you stay out of sight long enough, we can have a better chance to talk some sense into her."

Fiona did as her father suggested and retreated into her room. Her stomach was in such a knot. There was no spell that would have a chance at helping it at this point.

Vincent rose and opened the front door before Shyan even had a chance to knock on it. Brynn watched her father's expression as he looked into her mother's eyes. He looked as if he was in a dream state. He had been waiting for her to show up at his home for years and it was finally happening... even though on different terms than he had hoped for.

"Vincent..." Shyan's voice cracked at the sound of his name, and she began to cry. "Where is Fiona? Is she okay?"

"She is here, Shyan. Please come in. I assure you that I have been taking great care of her as well as Brynn."

Shyan walked into the house and sat down in the closest chair. She put her head into her hands and began to cry harder. She was talking, but it sounded like mostly gibberish with all of the sobs mixed in. All anyone really understood was the word "mistakes."

Brynn's anger at her mother began to fade

as she watched her deteriorating state. It was clear that she had become a very emotional and broken woman in the days since Brynn and her sister were forced to leave.

"Mom, there is something we need to talk about." Brynn said as she knelt on the floor in front of her mother.

Shyan looked at her with confusion and fear behind her tear-filled eyes.

"About your sister?" she somehow managed to choke out. "Is it worse than Drake said?"

"Mom, you are in danger. Do you really think that the Seelie court is going to sit idly by as your family becomes intertwined with vampires? Don't you think that they will see this all as a threat and come after you whether you are staying there or not?"

"What is this? Where the hell is your sister?" Shyan's whole demeanor changed, and Brynn stood up and backed away. The sadness in her eyes was beginning to change to anger and everyone knew that she was starting to see through the rouse. They had all hoped that she would feel so guilty about the choices she had made recently that she would listen to them. That hope was quickly turning to doubt.

Fiona opened her bedroom door and slowly made her way into the room. The fear on her face was visible to everyone.

"So, this was all just an elaborate hoax to get me to come here, is that it? Fantastic job, Vincent. I guess you figured that now that our children were with you, they could be used against me. I never came after all of the letters you sent me, and this was what, a last desperate attempt?"

Vincent became angry and a side of him that neither of the girls had seen before was coming out.

"Don't be so selfish, Shyan!" he shouted in a booming voice so powerful that shook the room. "This is not about me loving you. This is about trying to save our children's mother before the Seelie court makes you suffer for the decisions the rest of us have made. Do you really want Brynn and Fiona to spend the rest of their lives feeling guilty for what is certain to be your death? We have an informant inside of the compound and they reached out to us to warn us of the danger you are in. You cannot go back there. Don't you understand?"

Everyone in the room had completely stopped breathing as they watched the exchange between Vincent and Shyan in horror. The situation seemed to be spiraling downward too quickly to stop.

"You don't know what you are talking about Vincent. Girls, I am sorry. I hope you will both realize that. I cannot stay here. There are things that none of you know about. The Seelie court will not try to take action against me."

She rose to leave, and Vincent was in front of the door before she even took a second step.

"What *are* you doing?" she asked, sounding almost amused.

"I have already told you that you are not leaving. I do not wish to do anything by force, but I will."

"You can't stop me. I can cast a spell on

you if I need to."

"Shyan, just because I am a vampire does not mean that I am no longer a fairy." His massive wings appeared as soon as his sentence was finished. His golden curls bounced around as his wings fluttered.

"That... that isn't possible. They said..." Shyan couldn't even finish her sentence.

"They told you what? They said that because I was a child of the night, I would no longer be able to be a fairy. I should have known they would say that. And you have always bought in to any of the untruths that they have spewed your way. Of course, you believed them. This is all starting to come together."

"If you were still fae, why would they make you leave?"

"Because I was not *pure* any longer. They didn't want a half breed there making them look foolish to the other fairy clans. If they painted a picture of an evil demon, rather than the truth of what I was, then everyone would agree that I needed to be banished for the protection of the family. It has nothing to do with being fae and everything to do with how things are perceived."

Shyan sat back down in her chair. Vincent didn't move from the doorway.

"I believe that the Seelie court thought that one of the girls would tell you the truth about me. Our informant must have overheard something urgent enough to risk coming to us."

"Call him by his name. Your informant was Drake. We may as well talk about what he knows. He is almost here anyway. I know he was following me."

"That is good. We need to know everything that he knows. Fiona, why don't you go out and fetch him? He is your suitor after all. I'm sure he will be happy to see you."

She didn't have to be asked twice. She tried to hide the pep in her step as she headed for the front door. Vincent stepped to the side and let her go out. He walked over to the couch and took a seat next to Brynn. It appeared that he trusted Shyan not to leave at this point, at least not until they knew more.

"So, you still have all of your fairy abilities?" Shyan asked.

"Of course, I do. I do survive on blood now and I adhere to a vampire lifestyle for the most part. I haven't cast the daylight spell on myself in years. I have had no reason to not sleep during the day. Now that all of you are here, I might change that. It would make things easier. My baby vampire certainly seems to enjoy being able to walk in the day."

"*Your* baby vampire? Did you turn this poor boy into a vampire, Vincent?" Shyan looked disappointed and exasperated all at once.

"Yes, I did. Fiona came to me about the human boy that Brynn seemed to be in love with. I turned him in order to protect her from the court. He is the only vampire that I have ever made."

Before either of them could say anything else, Fiona and Drake appeared in the doorway.

"Drake, I presume. Thank you for taking such a risk to help my family." Vincent said as he reached his hand out to shake Drake's.

"It's not a problem. I just couldn't stand back and watch what they were doing to Fiona and her family. I am sick of the lies and the deceit. Everyone else on that compound might be a sheep, but not me."

"We need you to tell us exactly what you may know." Vincent motioned for Drake to take a seat.

"That's fine, but before I tell you anything, I need something from you. It won't be safe for me to go back there. Can I stay here with the rest of you? If you give me protection, I will tell you everything that I know. I'm a good fighter and I will earn my keep."

Vincent didn't exactly like the idea of his daughter's boyfriend living in the same house as her, but he guessed he was letting the same thing happen with Max. The circumstances were quite different, of course. Besides, Drake risked his own life to save Shyan's. She was here now because of him.

"Yes, you can stay here with us. I wouldn't turn you away. Just no funny business with my daughter. Now, let's talk."

"I was sneaking around near the

conference room. I was hoping to catch an earful of what happened to Fiona, since she had so suddenly disappeared. She would never leave without telling me goodbye. I knew something was up. I overheard them say something like 'She will surely find out the truth.' And 'Do away with her just like her disobedient sister.' I knew I had to warn you guys. So, I wrote that note and gave it to Brynn the next day. I remember learning about Shyan's sister being banished when I was younger. I had to try to intervene."

The mention of Madeleine visibly affected Shyan. She kept looking down toward the floor. She stared at the spiral pattern on the rug beneath her feet. Swirls of blue and grey stood out under the cream-colored armchair she was sitting in.

"All Madeleine ever did was love. She trusted them and thought that they would accept Coulter because she loved him. They knew that he had no intention of telling anyone about what we were. They killed her purely to set an example. They told everyone that she was banished, but I knew that she was dead. She would have tried to reach out to me otherwise. Even your letters made it to me, Vincent. Hers would have as well if she had ever tried to write any."

For the first time, Brynn realized that the address on the letters she saw in her mom's drawer wasn't Madeleine's. It was Vincent's. Why didn't it dawn on her when she came here? She must have been too overwhelmed to piece it all together.

No one in the room said anything. All this time, Brynn and Fiona had imagined that Madeleine was living somewhere far away from the reach of the court. They had always pictured her living in a cottage in the country. They both had assumed that the man she loved had been killed, but Madeleine was probably living alone. They never dared to think about the possibility of her being dead. Brynn had a brief surge of relief that Vincent had turned Max into a vampire. He really did save his life... for her.

"You are all right, I can't go back there. I must warn you, though, they will try to come after me. I know their secrets and fear that they will stop at nothing to silence me. My very presence here could put all of you in immense danger."

"What secrets do you speak of?" Vincent sounded genuinely curious, and Brynn was surprised that he did not already know. All eyes were on Shyan.

"Spell casting. When you cast a spell and bring something into existence, we all know that it cannot stay on this plane. Like that cat you inadvertently created that day, Brynn. You wanted to keep it, but I told you that it did not belong in this world. You cast it back to where it came from. The truth is that these creatures do not just disappear. They travel to a different plane."

"So, all of the things I have accidently conjured up over the years all exist somewhere?"

"Precisely."

"Why does this have to be a secret?"

"It is because the topic has much controversy surrounding it. Some of us believe that these creatures should be allowed to live out their lives, but others think that we should travel to that plane and hunt them down. There are even some members of the court who do in fact go and hunt. They make wagers and have contests on who can kill the biggest or most valuable game."

"Jesus Christ. How long have you known about this?" There was that angry, booming voice again.

"Vincent, I have known about this since I was a child. I overheard my father talking about it one day. He wanted to expose the ones who were participating, but he never got the chance. When he died, I vowed to finish what he had started."

"So, it is all one sick game to them?"

"I think it has progressed over the years. They may be intentionally creating beasts just to send them to the other plane. There have even been rumors of hunting people... perhaps some mystica factions. They might have prisoners. I do not know for sure."

"All of those years we were together. Why didn't you ever tell me? I could have helped you."

"Vincent, I don't know. I think part of me was trying to keep you safe and the other part needed to accomplish this on my own. If I knew then what I know now, I would have made different choices. It is what it is."

Everyone was shocked at the revelation. There was so much more going on than they could have possibly imagined. Brynn and Fiona began to feel a bit guilty about being so mad at their mother. She had just been trying to carry out her late father's wishes. Everyone in the room would probably have done the same.

"We won't let them get near you, Shyan. We can put up some protection wards tonight to keep us safe. No one will be able to get in here without an invitation. Kids, you can forget about school for now. It would be too easy for them to get to you there. That goes for you too, Max. You may not be a fairy, but you are part of this family just the same. They would go after you just like they would the rest of us."

Brynn tried not to smile at that last statement. She had often dreamed about Max being accepted into her family before she moved in with her father. It was not uncommon for fairies to marry young. She tried to imagine them getting married and having a ceremony where the people that she loved showed up to celebrate their union. Light blue flowers in her hair shimmering in the sun and Max's glistening golden eyes looking into hers. This was the first time that she ever felt that her daydream might be able to become a reality at some point. Max reached down, grabbed her hand, and gave it a squeeze.

"It will happen." He whispered into her ear, and she turned a bright shade of crimson. Shit. It was hard to remember that he was in her mind. She would have to find a spell to keep him from knowing what she was thinking. Her daydreams did have a tendency to border on embarrassing.

"Fiona and Brynn, you two will sleep together in Brynn's room tonight. If you don't mind showing Drake to your room Fiona, your mother and I will set up the protection wards. Max, there will be no training tonight so you can just hang out with the girls and Drake."

Everyone got up and headed toward the bedrooms.

TWELVE

"Let's cast some spells." Vincent reached his hand out for Shyan's, and he led her outside.

"Thank you." Shyan said in a soft voice when they were out in the yard.

"What are you thanking me for?

"For never giving up on me, even when

you definitely should have." Tears began to fall from her eyes, and she put her hand on his arm. She had forgotten how cold he was to the touch now that he was a vampire. Even though it was cold, it was comforting.

"I knew that you would come back one day, I just had to be patient. I knew that I would have my family back. After all of these years, Shyan, I have never stopped loving you. Hell, I haven't even entertained the thought of another woman. It was always you."

He hugged her tightly and he could feel her heart beginning to beat faster. It felt so good to hold her again. He didn't want to let go.

"Let's get the wards up and get back inside to the kids. You focus on the house, and I will focus on the rest." he said as he released her from his grasp.

He hadn't cast a spell in quite a while, so he hoped that he wouldn't be too rusty. He closed his eyes and pictured an invisible wall surrounding the property. He could see fairies trying to walk through it and being repelled. He focused his energy and continued to picture it. It shot up fifty feet high and closed on the top as if the entire property was being contained in a glass cube. Swirls of white swam through the lass, full of magic. It wouldn't be visible for long. Only until the magic solidified.

He glanced over at Shyan after his spell was done. She was still casting. Her eyes were closed for several more moments and he stood there just watching her. Despite her frazzled state, she was still just as beautiful as he remembered. She was still the woman of his dreams.

"All done, let's go in." she said as she looked up and saw his gaze. He smiled and followed her back into the house.

He locked the door behind them as Shyan began to close all of the blinds and curtains. She was surprised that he didn't have some sort of blackout device on the windows. She would have thought that he would want the whole house available to roam around during the day.

"Do you have another room for me to stay in or should I bunk with the girls?

"I thought that you could take my bed. It is downstairs." Shyan hesitated and he continued. "Don't worry, I will sleep on the couch. Let me show you." While he would love to share a bed, he wasn't going to push his luck.

He led her downstairs to his room. He had to guide her down the steps. It was too dark for her to get there on her own. Once they were on solid ground, he lit the candles on the top of his dresser.

"I was wondering where you slept since there is no sun protection upstairs. Speaking of that, would you like me to go ahead and cast the sunlight spell on you?"

"That's probably a good idea. It has been so long since I cast it, you will probably be more effective. It has always seemed safer to blend in with the other vampires. I also think..." he hesitated, not knowing how she might take his next suggestion. "That it might be a good idea for me to have a bit of your blood at some point. Don't freak out or anything. I know it is weird. It will make me be able to feel what you are feeling, and it will alert me if you are about to be in danger. I wouldn't suggest it if I didn't expect you to be in peril at some point." He hoped she didn't think that he was trying to pull one over on her. It really could help, and they needed all the help they could get right now.

She closed her eyes and put her hands on his arms. She pictured him out in the sunlight with her, like when they were young. She tried to swallow the lump that was growing in her throat. Her vision changed to them playing in the park with their girls. Everyone was so happy. It was the family experience they were robbed of. She cast the spell and opened her eyes.

"Why are you crying?" Vincent asked to her surprise. She didn't even realize that she was.

"I was just thinking about how things were before. It has been so long since I was with you... so long since I even let myself think about it. I thought by now I wouldn't feel anything for you, but that isn't the case. How is that possible?" She waved her hand in the air. "We can talk about it later. Let's sit down and get this blood thing over with. It kind of freaks me out, so hurry up and do it before I change my mind." She laughed as she wiped tears from her cheeks.

Vincent followed her to the bed and sat beside her. She closed her eyes, and he brushed her long shimmery hair away from her neck. She moved her head to the side, and he could see her pulse throbbing. He took a second to inhale her perfume before sinking his fangs in. He held her hand as she took a deep breath. Her warm blood filled his mouth along with a feeling he hadn't had since their last moments together.

He punctured his finger after retracting his fangs. He was about to rub his blood on the marks on her neck to make them disappear, but she stopped him.

"I want them to see. If they come for me, I want them all to see that this happened. I want them to know that they didn't win."

He would feel her heart beating. Desire began to run through his veins along with Shyan's blood. He felt intoxicated.

"You will never know how much I have missed you." He pressed his forehead to hers. "I have longed for the moment when I could reach out and touch you." Vincent whispered as he ran his fingers across her lips.

He didn't have a chance to say anything else before she pulled his face to hers and kissed him. Fourteen years of forgotten passion instantly surged through them. He tangled his hands in her beautiful blonde hair and they both fell backward onto the bed. The candles flickered as they continued to kiss. He was afraid that his strength might get the best of him and backed off a bit. Shyan pressed herself hard against him, not willing to stop what was starting and everything else seemed to fade away.

"Stop trying to listen, Fiona!" Brynn teased as she threw a pillow at her sister.

"I can't help it! What do you think is going on down there? Do you think that they are making up? I hope they aren't down there arguing or something."

"Maybe. Who knows?" Brynn smiled as her fingers intertwined with Max's.

"Where are you going to sleep tonight?" she asked him. "I don't think that you should go downstairs."

"I doubt that Drake wants a bed buddy, so I will probably just crash on the couch."

Drake laughed as he stretched out on the floor while playing footsie with Fiona. "You are definitely right about that dude. I would suggest swapping out roommates with Brynn, but I'm sure Vincent would kill me." He winked at Fiona.

"I know it isn't under good circumstances, but I am so happy that I don't have to go to school tomorrow. I don't know how Brynn put up with our shit for so long. People were so mean to me!" Fiona breathed a loud sigh of relief.

"Me too." Drake added. "I always thought it was lame that we had to go to public school. Everyone could tell we were different. Homeschool is popular these days, I always thought fairies should buy into that idea."

"Vincent says that it helps you guys learn how to blend into society." Max contributed.

"Yeah, but so can the playground and the mall." Drake laughed out loud.

"We should probably think about getting

some sleep. I'm sure we will have a busy day tomorrow." Max suggested.

Everyone agreed. Brynn and Fiona weren't very sleepy because of the spell that they had cast earlier to stay awake, but they could just cast a sleep spell to negate those effects. Drake excused himself to Fiona's room. He had a stressful day so he would need no sleep spell to help himself.

"I need something to drink, so I will walk with you to the couch." Brynn said to Max. Fiona waved goodnight as she crawled into her bed.

They walked together down the hall to the living room. Brynn grabbed the fleece blanket that was draped over one of the chairs and handed it to Max.

"I thought you needed something to drink."

"I do, but I really just wanted to spend some time alone with you. I should cast the sunlight spell on you before you go to sleep. It will be bright in here when you wake up."

"Good idea. I hadn't thought of that. I

wish we had a better idea of how long it lasts."

Max took off his shirt and shoes as he sat down on the couch. Since becoming a vampire, he had developed a rock-hard set of abs. They were good before, but this was on a whole new level. He caught Brynn looking at him and she blushed as she looked away. He smiled and stretched out.

She was surprised at the shape that he was in now that he was an immortal. She always thought that vampires would be pale and pencil thin, but Max's muscles were even more defined and enticing than she expected. It was hard to look away from him.

"Ready for the spell?" Max chuckled a bit. He had to admit, he was enjoying the way Brynn was looking at him.

Brynn nodded and grabbed his hands. She pictured the same thing that she had before. She saw them walking together in the park. The sun was shining high in the sky. They took a seat in the gazebo and enjoyed the feel of the warm summer day. She cast the spell and opened her eyes.

"That should do it." she said, not letting

go of his hands.

"So, are we going to talk about what you were thinking of earlier?"

"Huh?" she pretended to be confused, but she knew exactly what he was talking about.

"You were thinking about marrying me."

"I thought that you could only sense my emotions. Since when can you see my thoughts too?"

"That was the first time, I promise. Well, the second time. I saw everything when you cast the spell on me after you got me burned up." He laughed as he nudged her. He knew she was horrified when that happened, but enough time had passed. He could joke about it now.

"Perhaps it was because I was thinking the same thing." He said quietly.

She was lost for words. She just looked at him and smiled.

"My life became perfect when I met you, Brynn. Believe it or not, Vincent turning me into a vampire is the best thing that has ever happened to me. It means I will be able to spend hundreds of years with you. I love you, Brynn."

"I love you so much Max."

He pulled her onto the couch and kissed her. He could feel her desire inside of him. It was the most powerful thing that he had ever felt. It felt like his first day of school, his first kiss and Christmas morning all rolled into one. The passion they were feeling was so intense, they felt like they could ignite at any minute. His whole body was starting to tingle. He opened his eyes, and he was breathless.

"What's wrong?" Max had a look on his face that he never had before, and it made her nervous. He was looking at her like she had grown a second set of eyes or something.

"You skin is so shimmery. You should see yourself, Brynn. What just happened to you? Did you feel something change?"

She quickly got up and ran to the bathroom to look into the mirror. She couldn't believe what she saw looking back at her. She was beautiful. She shimmered just like the other fairies that she had always been jealous of. Even the color of her eyes was sharper. Her hair shined and the blue at the ends had turned to an almost electric color. She looked polished from her head down to her toes. It was like something had come alive inside of her.

She ran back into the living room and hugged Max.

"You are so damn beautiful." He said as he kissed her again.

His lips felt electric when they touched hers. She ran her fingers through his hair. She heard him groan and he pulled away suddenly. His fangs were out. He couldn't control himself.

"Do it." She said, surprising him.

"What?" Max panted, still feeling a bit breathless.

"I want you to feel what I feel, especially right now. No one has to know; you can cover the holes up."

She moved the hair away from her neck

and he pulled her close. He sank his fangs in without another thought. There was no resisting her. Her blood slid down his throat and he had never tasted anything so satisfying. It tasted different this time. It was sweet and almost intoxicating. Nothing like the metallic beverage he was getting used to. He let go of her neck and pierced his fingertip. He ran it over her wound and watched as it healed.

"How do you feel?" Brynn giggled softly.

"I feel like I just did some kind of drug. Your blood is different than it was before. This is crazy."

"Well, can you feel what I am feeling?" she asked shyly. Wondering if he would pick up on what she was trying to ask.

He pulled her back to him and began kissing her again. She wrapped her arms around his neck and moved as close to him as she could. He smelled so good. He must have sprayed on cologne when he woke up. She inhaled deeply, trying to memorize his smell.

Max pulled away suddenly and moved to the end of the couch at lightning speed.

"Fiona is about to come out here."

Brynn rubbed her hands over her hair and straightened her clothes. She tried to catch her breath. Max walked into the kitchen to wash the blood off of his mouth.

"Brynn, are you coming to bed?" Fiona asked sleepily.

"Yeah, I'll be right there. I'm just saying good night to Max." She said as her sister turned and walked back down the hall. She stood up to go check on Max.

Fiona closed the bedroom door and got back in bed.

"I'm surprised she didn't notice how shimmery you are. She must be really tired. You should go before she gets suspicious." Max suggested as he wrapped his arms around her waist, kissing her neck.

"Ugh, I don't want to. I had something else on my mind. You're probably right, though. Do you need a sleep spell or anything?"

"No. I'm pretty sleepy. It won't take me long to knock out. I'll see you in the morning, beautiful." He kissed her on the forehead, and she walked down the hallway to her bedroom disappointed that Fiona had interrupted them.

"What have you been doing?" Fiona asked, her back to the door where Brynn was standing.

"Fiona, I need you to turn on the light and look at me." She thought about waiting until the morning, but she was amped. Her sister needed to see this.

Fiona rolled her eyes. She thought that Brynn was being dramatic. She had already cast the sleep spell on herself, and she felt like her eyelids were about to slam shut.

"Whyyyy? I already cast the spell. I want to sleep."

"Come on. I promise you won't be disappointed."

Fiona sighed heavily and forced herself to turn over and face her sister.

"Holy cow! What happened to you? You look like a real fairy! I mean, you are a real fairy, but you have never had a shimmer like this before!"

"I know but keep your voice down. I don't want mom and dad to come up."

"So how did this happen? You are shinier than me!"

"I don't know. I was sitting on the couch making out with Max. He told me that he loved me and when he opened his eyes, I looked like this. It's like something inside of me just woke up or something. Have you ever heard of this happening before? I don't know what to think."

"That is crazy! You have always been different, though, so it's kinda par for the course for you. Maybe when you tell everyone else tomorrow leave out the making out part." She chuckled. "Now come to bed. I'm sleepy!"

Brynn smiled and turned off the light, hopping into bed. Adrenaline pumped through her body. She'd need that sleep spell tonight.

THIRTEEN

Brynn awoke to the smell of cinnamon rolls. She was still sleepy, but her hunger pangs were stronger. So, she sat up, jammed her feet into her fluffy blue slippers and headed out of her room.

"It's nice to see you in the daytime dad." Brynn said as she entered the kitchen. Vincent and Shyan smiled at each other.

Brynn didn't have to ask any questions. She knew that their love had been rekindled. There was nothing they could do to hide it. There was pure happiness in their eyes. Shyan had an expression on her face that Brynn didn't think she had ever seen before.

"Everyone look at Brynn!" Fiona shouted from behind her before anyone had a chance to look up and notice Brynn's new appearance on their own. She turned a bright shade of crimson. She hated being put on the spot.

"Thanks Fi." she said unenthusiastically.

"Oh my goodness, Brynn! Look at you! When did this happen?" Shyan asked in amazement.

"It started last night before I went to bed. I can't stop looking at myself." She giggled as she ran her fingers though her new shimmery hair. It even felt stronger, healthier.

"Do you know what may have caused it?" Vincent asked.

"I told her that I love her." Max chimed in as he entered the room. He was subsequently high fived by Drake.

Max walked over to Brynn and kissed her on the top of the head. She blushed again, embarrassed by all of her newfound attention. It was something that she was not used to. People usually just ignored her. That she could handle.

"So, what's on the agenda for today?" she quickly asked, hoping to change the subject. She grabbed a cinnamon roll and sat down at the table.

"I thought we could go to the diner. Max needs to feed today." Vincent suggested, sensing her discomfort. It was hard for Brynn not to blush. Max had healed her bite mark, so no one knew that he had already fed on her. The same could not be said for her mother, she noticed. You could clearly see the fang holes on her neck.

"I'm guessing you have already fed, huh?" Brynn joked as she motioned to her mom.

"Oh, you mind your business ma'am." Shyan snapped back, her cheeks becoming a bright scarlet red.

Everyone chuckled as they made their way downstairs. They were all surprised to see light in Vincent's quarters.

"Seeing as I have no problem with light now, I thought it may be easier for you all to navigate this place with more light."

He was right. This was the first time they hadn't been fumbling about, trying to find their way around down there.

The rest of the underground was still pretty dimly lit. They all followed behind Vincent. Brynn thought that she would remember the way to the diner, but she was completely lost. She glanced at Max and saw that he didn't seem to quite know where he was going either. That made her feel better.

"Have you ever been to this diner, mom?" Brynn asked, trying to make small talk.

"No, I haven't. I never strayed far from home. It was safer to not raise suspicions."

They arrived at the underground door. Vincent held it open as they all made their way inside. They found a booth big enough for all of them in one of the back corners. As they all took a seat, the same small werewolf girl from before brought them all menus.

"There is usually another fairy here." Vincent began speaking to Shyan. "I have never spoken to her so I don't know if you will know each other. I thought that if she were here today, you could chat. Maybe she will be useful to us."

"I doubt that I will know her. The only fairies outside of the family that I have met were traveling or passing through from afar. Maybe she will have heard some stories or something, though. It could be helpful. We could definitely use some more allies."

Their waitress came back, and they all put in their orders. Max wasn't really thirsty, but he ordered something that would suggest otherwise. He didn't know if it would be a big deal or not that he had more of Brynn's blood. Vincent had obviously fed on Shyan, but it was different. They were adults. Even though he was 18 and Brynn would be as well in a week or two, he knew they were still viewed as children. Everyone else picked food from the menu and Max was surprised when Vincent ordered a glass of blood as well.

"It's probably a good idea to stay full. It will keep my strength up just in case."

Max made a mental note. Vincent still hadn't taught him much about being a vampire. It wasn't really his fault at this point, there were a lot of bigger things happening at the moment. He had assumed that you should feed only when thirsty, but there was a definite correlation between staying full and being powerful. He would not forget that.

They were still waiting for their food when the mystery fairy came in through the front door.

"Perfect. There is the fairy I was telling you about." Vincent said to Shyan as he motioned to the front door.

Shyan turned to look at the fairy and their eyes locked.

"Shyan? Is it really you? What are you doing away from the compound?" The fairy swiftly made her way to the booth they were occupying.

Everyone was looking at Shyan for an explanation as to who the fairy was, but she didn't speak. She just sat there, staring at her. No one knew if she was confused or surprised.

"Is that you Madeleine?" Vincent was the first to speak. He knew who she was the second that he heard her voice. If only he had spoken to her when she was in there before. So much could have been different.

"Yes Vincent, it is me."

"It has been you all this time and I didn't recognize you. You look like a completely different person. How is this possible? Why didn't you speak to me?"

"I thought about it many times. I knew a bit about your situation, but I didn't want to take any chances. I would never have been able to forgive myself if something happened to Shyan or the girls because of me. When the court banished me, I fled to an alternate plane to hide. I knew that if they found me, I would surely die. They were out for blood. I met a warlock on my travels, and he helped me change my appearance. It has allowed me to survive all this time."

Shyan began to cry. She banged her closed fist on the table, rattling the silverware.

"All this time and you never once tried to reach out to me? I thought that you were dead! Do you know how long I grieved?"

"Shyan I am so sorry. You have to know that I wanted to, but it was too dangerous. They were so angry at me. They would have punished you for sure. I have been watching you and your family from a distance all this time. I couldn't risk your lives. What happened to me was bad enough."

Tears continued to fall from Shyan's eyes, but she said nothing more. It was hard to tell if she was angry or just overwhelmed. Brynn and Fiona just stared at Madeleine in wonder. She looked nothing like a fairy. Her hair was glossy and black with big curls. Her green eyes looked fierce through her thick black eyelashes. The only thing that was fairylike about her was her shimmery skin which seemed to have been dulled down.

"What about Coulter?" Vincent asked softly, afraid of what her answer would be.

"He was not as lucky as me. The court captured him. He was executed in front of me." She looked away as she wiped a tear from her cheek. "You will be in so much danger for talking to me, Shyan. The Seelie and Unseelie courts are in on this together. There is no one keeping the balance between good and evil anymore. There were elders there when Coulter died. They didn't do a damn thing to try to stop it. They just stood there and watched as he was slaughtered."

"I was in danger before I even saw you, Madeleine. I fled last night. They banished my daughters for dealing with vampires. A conversation was overheard that involved them getting rid of me like they did you. Until now, I thought that meant death."

"What are you going to do?"

"That's what we are hoping to figure out. All I know is that I plan to make them pay for what they have done to our family. This warlock you spoke of, do you keep in touch? Can he help us?"

"We have been together since the day he found me. He is the love of my life. I am able to live because of him. I can ask him to come speak with you. Are you all staying at Vincent's?"

"Yes, we are. We have protection wards up to safeguard it right now."

"That's a great idea. I doubt they would try anything out in the open, especially with vampires being in the house. That will frighten them. It is a good idea to be prepared, though. Who knows what they are willing to try to stop you from exposing them. I will go find Bruce and meet you in an hour. That will give you plenty of time to eat breakfast and start coming up with a plan."

"If we are not home when you two arrive, please let yourselves in." Vincent added.

Just as Madeleine glided away, everyone's food arrived at the table. They were all beginning to feel more than a bit anxious now, but it all looked too delicious not to dig in.

Vincent and Max finished their meals first, of course. It didn't take long to down a glass of blood. Everyone else was taking their time to actually savor their food. It was all very plentiful, and they needed to take advantage. They might not get the chance to run to the diner for food again anytime soon. Who knew what the courts were planning to do to them? Knowing that both courts were working together changed everything.

"Okay, I know I am the odd man out here, but can someone explain this court business to me? I thought that there was one court and I kind of made up my mind what it might be, but now there are apparently two? I'm lost." Max was going to wait until everyone was finished eating, but he needed answers.

"The fairies have two governing bodies if you will – the Seelie and Unseelie courts. The Seelies represent the good and the Unseelies the bad. Just like all other groups of people, there are bad fairies too. If the courts are working together for evil, the balance is lost. Nothing good can come of it." Vincent explained to his confused progeny.

"Ok, I think I get it now. Kinda."

Brynn smirked at Max as she swallowed the last bite of her sandwich. Everyone began to slowly rise and leave the table. They were a bit unsure of when Madeleine and Bruce would be arriving at Vincent's house. They didn't want to waste time and risk the wards causing problems for them. Fiona stretched before walking toward the door leading downstairs. Drake caught up to her and put his arm around her shoulders. She leaned her head into him and then descended the stairs.

Brynn was happy for her sister. The way she felt when she was with Max was the best feeling in the world and she was glad that Fiona was able to experience the same thing. Drake gave up everything to be with Fiona, just as Max had done for her.

She watched Max as he held her hand and led her back to their new home. He had such grace now that he was a vampire. He was light on his feet while still exuding a demeanor of power. She could easily be addicted to the feeling of being near him.

"Your aunt is already here." Max whispered to Brynn.

She was about to ask him how he knew, but then she remembered his great senses. He could probably smell Madeleine long before he mentioned it.

"At least she didn't get held up by the wards. I hope that doesn't mean they aren't working properly. Maybe they can sense your intentions or something. Is Bruce with her?"

"Yes."

"What does he smell like?"

This was going to be the first warlock that they encountered. She was curious how his smell might differ from the other beings that Max had described to her the last time they were at the diner.

"It's a little hard to describe... very different. Kind of woody, with hints of herbs. It's a very clean smell."

As they reached the door to their new house, she began to get butterflies in her stomach. She had never met a warlock before. She was so hopeful that Bruce would be able to help them. She just got her mother back. She wasn't about to lose her again. She wanted her to be able to live in peace and enjoy her life with her family. That was something the court had stolen from her long ago. It was something that she deserved. They all did.

As Vincent opened the door, everyone poured into the basement. The familiar flicker of the candle on the dresser had been replaced by the dim light from the lamp. It was a convenience that Vincent was enjoying for the first time in a long time. The day walker spell was magnificent. While artificial light did not have negative effects on vampires like sunlight did, not relying on it made life out of the sun easier. He led his family upstairs in search of Madeleine and her warlock counterpart. He found them sitting on the couch in the living room. They were discussing something but stopped speaking when everyone entered the room.

"I'm glad you came so soon." Shyan said when she saw her sister. Her voice sounded genuine, but there was still a hint of resentment. She was thrilled that Madeleine was still alive. There was a part of her, though, that couldn't help but feel a bit burned by the fact that Madeleine had never tried to contact her in any way after being banished. They had always been so close. She spent so many years mourning a loss that didn't even occur.

"Everyone, this is Bruce." Madeleine said as everyone filtered into the room.

Bruce rose from his seat to greet everyone. He wasn't very tall in stature. He was rather stocky, which made his lack of height more noticeable. The hair on his head was fluffy and a multitude of shades of grey. It was messy, though he looked to be well groomed otherwise. His beard was grown out to match the rest of him. He wore an amulet around his neck adorned with many different gemstones. His most captivating feature was his eyes. They were a piercing shade of blue. His pupils were very catlike, which was common of warlocks, or so Brynn had read in books growing up.

She didn't know much about warlocks in general. She learned a bit about them when she was younger. They were believed to be evil for lack of a better word. Their motives were usually a bit sinister, and their magic was much more powerful than that of a fairy. Wands were not a tool commonly used by warlocks, but herbs and crystals were often utilized. They never used weapons. They relied solely on magic. They could summon creatures and even more.

"It is very nice to meet you all." Bruce began. "Madeleine has been filling me in on the details of the mess you are in. I am here to offer my full support. I helped Maddie in the other realm once before, so I believe I will be of beneficial use to you. Have you come up with any plans yet?"

Everyone just looked around at each other, not wanting to admit just how unprepared they were.

"Other than going to the realm, not much has been formulated yet." Shyan spoke up. She was surprised that Bruce didn't look disappointed.

"That is great. We will have fresh ideas, then. Let's get started."

Pleased with Bruce's optimism, everyone filed into the living room and took a seat. Brynn and Max picked a spot on the floor in front of Fiona and Drake who were on the couch. Brynn leaned her head back against Fiona's legs. She enjoyed feeling like she had a real sister, not just someone who was disappointed to be related to her. It was a pleasant change.

"Perhaps we can start by deciding on what role each person here will play. I do not know you all very well, so I will leave those decisions up to you. What are everyone's strengths?"

"Max and I will fight, of course." Vincent spoke up. "I think Brynn and Shyan should fight with us. Our connections with them are deep enough that we will be able to easily sense when they are about to be in any real danger."

"Brilliant. Perhaps you two can consume a portion of their blood leading up to the fight. As pairs, you could be unstoppable. It would even be good to make that a regular habit until then. Not necessarily every day, but more than once would be ideal. I will need another person to help me cast. Who would that person be?"

"I'll do it." Drake volunteered. "I've never been good with any kind of battle skills, but I am a great caster."

"That leaves Madeleine and Fiona. Madeleine knows the realm better than all of us. She should definitely be our guide." Vincent turned to Fiona. "What do you think you would be best at?"

"I don't know..." Fiona pondered. "I think I am better at casting than fighting, but I am up for either."

"If Drake and I concentrate on the portal and protection spells, perhaps you could stay close to those in battle and focus your energy on restoration spells and things of that nature."

Bruce's suggestion was great, and Fiona was excited about it. She would never admit it, but the thought of battle did frighten her a bit. Not because she was afraid of those who were the enemy, but she was scared that others would get hurt trying to help her. She felt somewhat responsible for the mess they were in.

They all decided that the next step was to practice their craft. Bruce agreed to take Drake and Fiona under his wing and teach them everything he knew about the spells they would need to be casting. Drake would have to learn how to create and help protect the portal that they would have to use. Fiona needed to know how to cast better restore and repair spells.

"Madeleine, can you tell us what you saw when you were on the other plane?" Vincent asked. She could have a wealth of information that would prove to be very valuable to them.

"I have heard so many terrible rumors since dad's death. I hope that they cannot be true. They have progressively been getting worse over the years." Shyan piped in.

"Without even knowing what you heard, I can guarantee that they are all true. It is truly a terrible place. They have prisoners in cages - wolves, shifters, you name it." Madeleine said solemnly.

Everyone gasped as they realized the horror was real.

"That's why Bruce was there. A warlock had gone missing, and he heard the rumors surrounding the fairy plane. He didn't find the warlock in question, but he did find me."

"How did you spend time there without the court getting to you?" Brynn was captivated by the story.

"They are only there on hunting days or when they are bringing in new prisoners. They sent me there when I was first banished. They let me roam on my own for a while. I think that they wanted me to see the evil that they were capable of before they killed me. I am just lucky that Bruce got me out of there before then."

"Well then, at least we know everything we are fighting for is justified. We have to put a stop to this and avenge our family." Vincent stood. "Let's start working toward our goal, guys."

Madeleine headed for the kitchen to sit down and draw a map. She had spent enough time in the other realm that she would be able to depict every inch of it. It was permanently imprinted on her brain. The rest of them left to practice fighting.

FOURTEEN

Vincent didn't like the idea of a vampire feasting on his daughter, even if it was a vampire that he created. He knew that it was for the best, though. It would give Brynn much better protection during the fight, and he knew that Max would die to save her. Still, it was like opening Pandora's box to lustful feelings. Kids their age didn't need any more temptation than they already had.

"At least we don't have to hide it anymore." Max whispered into Brynn's ear as he pushed the hair away from her neck. She giggled as she closed her eyes. She took a quick, deep breath as he sunk his teeth in.

It was getting less painful each time that he bit her. She didn't know if her getting used to it was a good thing or a bad thing. All she knew was that she loved how close and connected it made them feel.

Vincent kept himself too busy feeding on Shyan to watch what was going on with his daughter. By the time he was finished, Max and Brynn were laughing audibly. He was happy to know that Max was finished as well. This was all new to him and a bit awkward at that. He hoped that he would get used to it enough to not be bothered by it. It was more helpful to Brynn than it was dangerous or destructive. He had to keep that in mind.

Now that he and Max had all the blood that they needed to be at the top of their game, they practiced fighting. Because he was older than Max, he would be faster and stronger than him. He was definitely physically stronger than any fairy, so if Max could keep up with him, a fairy would be easy to take out.

"Max and I will go first. You girls watch us and take notes of any weaknesses that you see."

Vincent made a hand motion to Max as if to say, "come and get me." Max ran at Vincent with all his might. Right before he was about to deliver his first blow, Vincent jumped high into the air sailing over Max. He landed on his feet and spun around. Max had already started jumping into the air to catch him. Vincent anticipated Max's attack and brought him down with one arm. Max landed hard in the dirt. A cloud of dust rose around him. Brynn was pretty certain that his impact made the entire planet shake.

"You're going to have to do better than that if you plan to lay a hand on me." Vincent laughed pompously, hoping to anger Max.

His taunting must have worked because Max took a huge leap and before Vincent knew it, Max's feet were on his chest, pushing him to the ground. A patch of grass was torn from the earth and Vincent landed on his back, sliding a bit before he came to a rest. With a smile, he grabbed Max's feet and slung him at least thirty feet across the yard.

"Weak points? Concerns?" Vincent asked Shyan and Brynn as Max walked back over to join them.

"That was quite a show. Thank God these protection wards also keep people from seeing what is taking place on this property. A little glitz and glamour can go a long way to make this look like a normal, boring human yard." Shyan commented as she began to ponder something.

"The fairies will have no hope of beating you in a physical match one on one. I do think we will be outnumbered, though. There will be more than four of them to fight. If only we had more people to help us. I don't know that we can make it otherwise."

"Do you have anyone in mind?"

"No. I don't really know anybody outside of the fairy world. I was hoping you might know some people."

"I know a few other mystica, but I don't know that they would care about our fight. They are mostly shape shifters and they generally stay out of the business of others. They are a tough bunch but are overall pretty peaceful."

Brynn and Max looked a bit surprised. Perhaps the people that Max couldn't identify in the diner that day were shape shifters. Neither of them had ever heard of such a thing. They were both instantly filled with questions, but they would have to wait for a more appropriate time.

"We should at least ask them. The worst that they can say is no. If they say yes, then we would have a strong advantage. The court may expect vampires to show up in the realm, but they would never anticipate having to fight a shifter. They rarely even acknowledge their race. It would throw their game off."

Vincent agreed with Shyan. He wasn't optimistic, though. While he might call these shifters his friends, they had never really helped him with anything in the past. They strongly believed that staying out of the affairs of others is what had kept them all alive for so long. He would need a strong bargaining chip to persuade them to help out.

"Look alive princess. I guess it is our turn." Shyan turned to say to Brynn.

Brynn was nervous about practicing with her mom. The only kind of fighting she had done before was a few moves with a dagger. They weren't using weapons on each other, so she didn't know what exactly her mother had planned. Everyone had written her off for so long that no one invested the time to teach her anything important about survival.

"I'm sure you are curious as to what we are going to do. Since we are relying on the others to cast the spells for us during battle, we will be relying on hand-to-hand combat. I know you have had some practice with a blade, so that will be helpful. I am going to teach you some non-weaponry skills today. We will need to practice with our wings out. They will be out during battle, so we may as well get used to it now." Shyan chuckled as she saw the uncertainty on Brynn's face. "Trust me, baby girl. That fluff won't weigh you down as much as you think it will.

Shyan knew that Brynn would be good with a dagger, so she decided to show her some martial arts self-defense moves that she learned from Krav Maga. The first move was how to get away if someone puts you in a bear hug. Shyan wrapped her arms around Brynn and instructed her to grab her nose with the right hand and pull her mom's face away from her body. With her left hand she needed to deliver a good blow to the chin. Brynn was scared that she was going to hurt her mom, but they practiced in slow motion at first. She was thrilled when she was able to take her mom down to the ground.

They went over a few elbowing and arm-twisting techniques before taking a break. They both wished that they had the endurance of vampires right now. As it was, they were sweating heavily and chugging water. Brynn batted her wings to create a breeze to help cool her off. This time her giant angel wings were coming in handy. And her mom was right, they weren't weighing her down. If anything, she felt like they were helping her somehow.

"Those were mighty impressive moves Shyan." Vincent said with a grin. "Where did you learn all of that?"

"You can find anything on the internet. It might be helpful if you practiced with Brynn. She won't be able to hurt you, so it would be good practice now that she knows the moves. She needs to try to fight without fear of hurting me."

Max volunteered, but Vincent feared that he would take it too easy on Brynn. If she had any hope of successfully fighting someone, she needed to be challenged. Brynn was nervous at the thought of fighting her father, but she agreed after he promised not to use any "sneaky vampire moves" as she called it.

As soon as his massive angel wings came out, she knew it was time to fight. It was truly a sight to see, both of them with their giant wingspans. It was beautiful. He started by lunging at her and putting her in a bear hug. You would think that would be a difficult move with wings, but it was surprisingly easy to maneuver. Her adrenaline was pumping hard. She had definitely underestimated the force that he would use. He was not going easy on her. She struggled for a moment and tried to regain her footing. Once she had that down, her instincts took over. With one swift move, she grabbed his nose and pulled with all her might. She didn't even have time to hit him before he fell away from her. He stumbled for a few steps but left her no time to gloat about her victory.

Suddenly he was behind her with his arm around her neck. His speed was remarkable, and he wasn't leaving her any time to anticipate his moves. She dropped her weight to the ground and came loose from his grip. She seized her opportunity on the ground and gave him an elbow to the foot. It allowed her time to slip away from him completely.

"Very impressive my girl. You learn quickly. If you could keep up with *my* speed, I have faith that you will be able to take on a fairy."

Brynn smiled at her father's encouraging words. If someone had told her a week ago that she would be play fighting with a vampire in preparation for a battle, she would have tried to have them committed. But that was her life now. Her days of being awkward and ridiculed were far behind her. She had evolved into a strong and confident fairy. Yes, it was a quick transition, but it happened, nonetheless.

"I'm so proud of you." Max said as he began picking little white feathers out of her hair. "Everyone is going inside to regroup. Think they would notice if we were missing for a bit?" He kissed her neck and slid an arm around her waist.

Brynn giggled as she began to blush. Max held her there for a moment more. She stared into his blazing gold eyes. He could feel the heat of desire coming off of her body. Feeling her urges was such a powerful thing. It was hard to resist the things that it made him want to do.

"Let's go inside before I can't resist you any longer." Brynn said with a smile, grabbing Max's hand and leading him into the house. Thank God she had self-control. He was definitely losing his.

Brynn was surprised to see unfamiliar faces sitting inside when they arrived. No one tried to come in through the front while they were practicing. Plus, Max usually alerted her to who was coming and going. He must have really been distracted.

"It's about time that the two of you joined us." Madeleine said, ushering them inside. I would like you to meet a few people."

Brynn shifted her attention to the three strangers sitting on the couch. The two men looked very similar. They both had wavy, dirty blonde hair with hazel eyes and had a fairly large build. They looked to be covered in nothing but pure muscle and tattoos. The woman sitting between them was petite with long, jet black hair and thick straight cut bangs. She shared the same hazel eye color as the men. She wished that she had the same sense of smell that Max had now. She had no idea who these people were, but they had to be supernatural.

"Brynn and Max, meet Raef, Gideon and Quyen." They each gave a nod in the direction of their visitors.

"We are shape shifters." Quyen said with a sense of amusement, her head tilted to the side. Realizing that she was staring, Brynn blushed and quickly looked away.

"Sorry to stare. We have never met any

shape shifters before. To be honest, I didn't even know they existed until today." Max explained.

"No apologies necessary, young vampire. We are here to help you guys out." One of the men responded. Brynn wasn't sure who was Raef and who was Gideon. Maybe they were twins. They had to be brothers at the very least.

"No offense, but why would you want to help us? I mean, I am glad to have you, but what do you want with a fairy fight anyway?" Brynn hoped she hadn't been rude, but she was curious. She felt like her guard had to be up at all times now. Could they trust these people?

"It isn't just fae folk in that realm that you are planning on going to. Fairies have tricked our kind into being stuck there as well." Quyen looked down at her hand that were folded neatly in her lap. "My father, their uncle (she motioned to Raef and Gideon), was tricked by a female fairy named Tabya years ago. He thought that they were in love, and she convinced him to move in with her. He didn't realize until it was too late that she was just a minion of the Unseelie court. He has been trapped there ever since, unable to escape from the power of their spells." She tried to blink away the tears welling up in her eyes. One of the men put his hand on her knee.

"I'm sorry. I had no idea how far they had really gone. I am honored to have you fight with us." Brynn said somberly. If there was one thing that she understood, it was father issues. She would like to do anything to help Quyen get her father back.

"We are indeed lucky to have them by our side. Raef and Gideon can shift into a lion and bear, respectively. Quyen can become the deadliest panther you have ever seen. They will be tough to go up against. It would be a definite advantage for us." Madeleine boasted, which gave Brynn the impression that she was the one to recruit them.

"Well, we had no doubts about helping once we heard about Brynn." Quyen said with an expression that Brynn couldn't quite put her finger on.

"What about me?" Brynn laughed a little

nervously. Her presence should be the last reason for anyone to want to help them. Things might be a little better for her now, but she still felt like she was on the front row of the struggle bus.

"We shifters have a prophecy that speaks of the day that we will stand up and fight against those who persecute us. We will fight side by side with other mystica allies. The one to lead us is said to be a young fairy. She is a special fairy, purer than the rest. That can be noted by the difference in her wings. The time to fight is marked by a significant change in her. When we heard that your appearance had changed, we knew that you were the one."

Brynn didn't know what to say. Her changed appearance did surprise her, but she had just assumed that Max had something to do with it. Surely they had made some kind of mistake. She definitely wasn't part of any prophecy. She could barely cast spells. There was a logical explanation as to why she finally started looking like a fairy. It could have been stress, excitement, or two million other things. She didn't have to know what the answer was for there to be one. It just was.

As Brynn looked around the room, she realized all eyes were on her.

"You guys don't believe that prophecy is really about me, do you? Come on, there is no way. I can barely make fairy dust! In fact, I have only made it once. Every other time it has just been dirt!" She felt herself getting defensive, but she didn't know how to stop.

"I believe it to be true." Vincent said while shaking out his wings. Brynn hadn't noticed that they were still out until now. Hers were still out too for that matter. They had nothing to hide here, so there was no reason to conceal them. It was more comfortable not to anyway. She had kept them put away when she lived at the fairy compound, but that was just because people teased her for having angel wings instead of the normal fairy wings.

"Dad, you can't be serious."

"You have always been special, Brynn. Just look at your wings."

"You have the same wings as I do, dad. What's so special about that?"

"I think it is time for us to have a little

family history lesson." He motioned for everyone to take a seat. Brynn hesitated but complied.

"The fairy race is nothing more than fallen angels who have not lost their heavenly powers. When we were cast out of heaven, there was only one family that was allowed to keep their original wings. There was a reason for that - they were chosen. The agreement being that as long as they kept a watchful eye on the rest of the race and intervened when necessary, they wouldn't lose their original wings and a few other abilities. They would fight for justice in order to keep their heavenly ties. Their purity. That family is ours, Brynn. We have been protecting other fairies from the beginning of our kind's existence."

"Why doesn't Fiona have angel wings?"

"It is like any other kind of hereditary feature... some get passed on and some don't. Only one other of my siblings was born with angel wings as I was. This is why I know that the shifter prophecy is true. Your blood is that of a fighter, a protector of our kind. There is no one else that this prophecy could be about."

Brynn was quiet for a moment. Vincent couldn't tell if she was feeling empowered or just overwhelmed. He did feel slightly bad for making Brynn's purpose sound so magnificent and honorable when Fiona didn't have the same obligations. Her heritage wasn't any less noble than that of Brynn's, but the wings came with a destiny to fulfill.

Brynn began to tear up. With everyone's eyes settled on her, she couldn't contain the feelings building up inside of her any longer. It wasn't fair to put this kind of pressure on her.

"This is idiotic! If your 'chosen one' is a girl who has only been casting spells right for a week, then that is just ridiculous." She ran out of the house to the front yard, warm tears still streaming from her eyes.

Max made a motion for the door, but Vincent's hand on his shoulder stopped him. Without a word Vincent vanished from sight, leaving everyone else in the room still sitting in silence.

"I'm sorry, I should have handled that better." Brynn said quietly when she felt Vincent put his arm around her shoulders.

She felt so devastated and embarrassed.

"I always thought that the story of our family was nothing more than hokum." Vincent began to speak softly to Brynn. "Then one day when I was young, while we were eating dinner, a man came to speak with my father. He apologized that he had to part in the middle of supper and left with his visitor. I had never seen the man before, but I knew he must be family because he had the same wings as my father and I did. That was the last time I ever saw my father.

My mother told me that there was a group of fairies casting spells on young women. They were tricking them into doing unthinkable things and then killing them. My father and a few others from our family had to stop them. He and his brother were both killed in battle. That is when I knew the legend was true. The man who came for my father, who I later learned was a cousin, shimmered more that I had ever seen in a fairy before. He shimmered just like you, Brynn. I know that this is a lot to take in, but you can't hide from your destiny."

"Why didn't anyone tell me this before

now? All this time I thought that I was just some freak with the wrong wings. A mistake. Do you know how much easier my differences would have been to handle if I knew it was for some sort of higher purpose? My whole life has been hard because of it."

"I do know, because that was the only thing that made it easy for me when I was growing up. I think that deep down, your mother didn't fully believe any of it. The story of our family is that of secret. It would have caused such jealousy if everyone knew that our family was chosen and theirs was not. So, no one is ever told of how special we are. Your mother knew because I told her what I was, of course. She thought it was some hoax that I cooked up and then you were born with angel wings. It frightened her that the stories could be true. Sometimes things go away if you don't speak of them. Besides, all of the trials that you have been put through over the years are just going to make you a stronger fighter. It has made you a stronger person. It had to be this way."

"I should just let those jerks back home deal with this themselves. They would deserve it after how they have treated me all of this time…"

Brynn paused a moment, as if she was pondering something. She let out a sigh as she closed her eyes and rubbed her temple.

"If I am supposed to lead this thing, there is a lot that you are going to have to teach me. As of right now, I am a shitty fairy and that is going to get us all nowhere fast."

"I intend to my dear." Vincent said with a chuckle as they turned to walk back inside.

"Do you really think I can do this?"

"I wouldn't be encouraging it if I didn't. I'm not just hyping you up because you're my daughter. This prophecy… this isn't the first time I have heard about it. I do not know all of the details. In fact, I don't know most but I have always believed that it was about you. I just didn't know how everything would fall into place. Come on my fairy queen, our guests are waiting on us."

Everyone looked up when Brynn and Vincent returned. She blushed, feeling embarrassed but she refused to look away. She had to start facing things.

"So, are you in?" Quyen asked in a tone that suggested it was something that she needed to happen.

"Yeah, I'm in. Let's get this figured out."

She sat down and everyone began to discuss their ideas, strengths, and weaknesses. It was a good discussion and after everything was said and done one thing was clear. They needed a bigger team.

The shifters went home with the promise of returning the following day. Having them there made Brynn hopeful, but she was relieved when they went home. The whole discussion left her feeling exhausted. She couldn't wait to lose her eyes and leave everything behind for a while.

*   *   *

She could hear footsteps coming up behind her. The changing of the seasons had ushered in a crunchy forest floor. No one could be stealthy out here right now.

"There you are Fairy Queen. I thought I might find you in our woods." He kissed the top of her head.

Brynn looked down and saw herself. She was wearing a flowy white floor length dress. She felt the crown upon her head. The moon lit up the meadow she was standing in.

"Do you think something bad is about to happen? I can't shake the feeling. If they are working together, we're in big trouble."

"We can't change what is already in motion. We know that, even without the prophecy pointing it out."

"You're right. I just think there must be something I could do to change something. This is all happening because of me."

"That might be partially true. Even so, you can't blame yourself for someone turning to the dark side. It doesn't happen unless the thought was already there... waiting in the back of this mind the whole time."

Brynn nodded but said no more. She closed her eyes and focused on the breeze that was blowing through her hair. She could stop *something bad from happening. She was confident of that. The question remained... should she?*

FIFTEEN

Brynn's body was so sore when she awoke the next morning that she would have sworn that she had been hit by a truck. She didn't know how she was going to get out of bed. Not to mention, she couldn't get that dream off of her mind. Did it mean something? And who was the guy that she was with? She never got to see his face.

"I can fix that." Fiona chirped, sensing that Brynn was hurt by her moan and grunts. "I practiced a lot of healing and restoring spells yesterday."

"Have at it. I will happily be your guinea pig today." Brynn said with a smile and open arms, happy that she didn't have to concentrate on casting a spell so early in the morning.

She watched as Fiona closed her eyes and began to concentrate. She wondered what kind of spell she was going to cast. They were sure to teach Fiona some powerful spells if she was expected to keep them all safe during battle. Fiona stretched her arms out wide, took a deep breath and put her hands on Brynn's arms. She immediately had a surge that felt like heat and relief run down her arms throughout the length of her body. It was a sensation that she had never felt from a spell before.

"And just like that, you are healed." Fiona squeaked as she kicked her leg up behind her, clearly excited to have tried her spell for the first time.

"That was incredible. I have never felt something so powerful from a spell before. They must have been teaching you some good ones yesterday."

"Madeleine and Bruce showed me some amazing things yesterday. There are spells I am learning that I would never have been able to comprehend before. It's so exciting!"

Brynn smiled. After Vincent's history lesson yesterday, she was afraid that Fiona would feel left out of something special. It was good to see that she did have an important way to contribute. Despite their differences in the past, she didn't want anything to interfere with their newfound relationship.

"So, do you know what is on the agenda for today?"

"I'm not sure. I assume that Drake and I will be learning more spells. Do you think that you and mom will practice more fighting moves? How was it yesterday?"

"It was fun I guess, but also kind of weird. I don't know. I really want dad to teach me a few spells or something. That is my weakness right now. I don't know if I will have to cast during battle or if I am just fighting. Either way, I feel like if I don't have any spells in reserve I will be massively lacking. It's always good to have a backup plan."

The girls finished getting dressed and ready to go meet the others. Brynn didn't know if she should dress for battle or not, so she just threw on some comfortable jeans and a tank top. It would give her room to move around if she needed to. Fiona chose a very typical pink dress and sandals.

"You're such a girly girl" Brynn said to her as they both giggled and walked down the hallway.

As usual, everyone else was already up and congregated in the kitchen. Brynn was still amused at the fact that the kitchen was Max's favorite hangout even though he no longer ate food. He was sitting at the table chatting with Drake when she and Fiona walked in.

Drake greeted Fiona with a smile and a kiss. She blushed and turned her head to the side. "Not in front of everyone babe!" she giggled.

Brynn made her way to the table and grabbed a muffin. She took a seat on Max's lap and began to eat.

"Good morning." he said as he tucked her hair behind her ear.

"Have you seen my parents yet this morning?" Brynn asked, noticing they were absent from the breakfast festivities.

"Yeah, they went to the diner looking for new recruits. They said to make sure everyone has a good breakfast to fuel up for today's work. Sounds like it's gonna be a big day."

Brynn wondered what was in store for her today as she finished eating her muffin. She got a nervous feeling in the pit of her stomach. She felt like she was going to battle any day, but they were all so unprepared. She had to trust in her family and friends now. Together they could free themselves.

As she took her last bite of muffin, she heard footsteps and the door. She turned to look at Max.

"There are new people with them. They smell like wolves."

She loved that he could always give her a heads up on who to expect. Those vampire skills were something to be admired.

"And what do wolves smell like exactly?"

"Like a combination of dog and dirt. What did you expect?"

"That is what I expected, I guess." She laughed. "That's good that we have more help."

Vincent and Shyan led their new friends into the house. Just as Max said, there were werewolves. Three of them to be exact. What he failed to mention was the other vampire that was with them.

"We are back with reinforcements." Vincent announced loudly.

"This is Daveson, Finn and Patrick." He motioned toward the wolves. They nodded, but everyone was clearly more interested in who the vampire was.

"The gentleman that you are all staring at is Gautier. He is my maker."

You could have heard a pin drop. All this time Brynn had assumed that Vincent did not have a relationship with his maker. She had envisioned him becoming a vampire in such a violent way that he would want to cast away anyone that caused it to be.

"Hello, everyone. I am honored to fight with you all. It would mean a lot to me to help bring vengeance to the people who have caused Vincent such pain over these years."

Gautier had an accent that Brynn couldn't place. It sounded ancient and unfamiliar. He did look like a fighter. His pale skin did not mask the muscles that she could see outlined underneath his shirt. What was up with these good bodied vampires? His sandy brown hair hung down close to his eyes. His clothes were surprisingly trendy for someone who was probably a few hundred years old.

"The sunlight doesn't bother you, huh?" Fiona asked with a mouthful of food.

"No, young fairy, it does not bother me. Your mother was kind enough to help me with that... setback. I will say, after being in the darkness for hundreds of years, this is quite fascinating... and bright." He laughed to himself.

"What do we do now?" Brynn asked no one in particular.

"Our friends from yesterday are all on their way here. Once they arrive, we can begin making plans." Shyan said as she walked into the kitchen and grabbed a muffin. Her trip to the diner this morning had not been for food, and she was starting to feel it. "I suggest you all fuel up because we will be busy once everyone is here."

Everyone did as she suggested and finished eating breakfast. Brynn had so many thoughts fluttering in her mind. Everyone else probably did too for that matter. Vincent handed Max a cup and told him to drink up. He must have gotten blood to go while he was looking for recruits. Weird, but thoughtful. Brynn wanted him to have all of the blood he could get his hands on. It would make him stronger, and she wanted to be sure he was coming out of the battle on top. She was not ready to say her goodbyes to him or anyone else for that matter.

Madeleine, Bruce, and the shifters that they met the day before showed up just as they had finished eating. Madeleine was wearing a worried expression and just the look of it made Brynn wish that she hadn't eaten. Her stomach was instantly in knots.

"I know this is fast, but we need to finalize our plans today. We have it on good authority that the courts are about to make their move. If we want any chance at an upper hand, we must strike first and catch them off guard."

"How did you come about this information?" Vincent sounded as if he was trying to mask the worry in his voice.

"I have been keeping an eye on their realm. I peeked in once we left here last night and there was much activity all about. They know that we are up to something. I could not tell what they are trying to plan or organize, I just know that we need to strike quickly while we still can." Bruce said with a steady and convincing tone.

"Ok everyone, you heard the man. Let's get our shit together. Drake must learn how to open the portal today. Madeleine, if you are done drawing the map, amp up the spell casting with Fiona. Brynn and Max let's go battle with the rest of our friends. After a few hours, let's all reconvene inside and map out exactly what our plan is once we get there." Vincent barked out orders like he had been doing this all his life. Everyone listened and did as he said. His voice was so commanding. You had no choice but to listen.

Brynn was nervous about practicing with their new friends. She knew the logistics of fairies and vampires, but these mystica were a whole new ball game. She didn't know about their strengths or skills. She had no idea what to expect and she didn't want to feel helpless and inexperienced in comparison.

Vincent suggested that they practice with someone that they didn't really know. It would encourage them all to learn new skills or habits they wouldn't otherwise have known about. Gideon offered to pair up with Brynn. Max paired up with one of the wolves and after that Brynn lost focus on who was fighting who.

"I know this is stupid, but do I fight you as a man or as a bear?" Gideon laughed heartily at her question.

"You can have the man right now. I can't stop myself from hurting you as easily once I am a bear. Claws and whatnot."

Brynn smiled and her nervousness began to ease up a bit. She appreciated his kindness.

"Ok fairy, show me what ya got." He said with a wink as he planted his feet in a steady position.

He charged at Brynn and tried to grab her. She used every Krav Maga skill that she had. It was better than fighting Vincent. That vampire speed was hard to keep up with. Gideon was much stronger than she would ever be, but at least he was more her pace. She got in a few good punches before he got the upper hand and laid her flat on her back. She panicked. His weight was far too much for her to push off and it just left her scrambling underneath him. He wasn't getting up. She felt trapped. He smelled like cinnamon and the scent filled her nose as she was trying to figure out what to do.

"Stop panicking for a second." Gideon

said, still on top of her. "This is actually quite easy for you to get out of. If anybody has you on your back and you want them off, you have two options. First, you can kiss them. They would be surprised, and you could get the upper hand." He laughed at the joke he had just made, but Brynn was not as amused as he was. It made her oddly nervous. "In a battle setting, though, you just need to start flapping your wings. With big, beautiful wings like those, you will be out of this situation in no time. Give it a try and see what I'm talking about."

That was an option that had never crossed her mind. She stared at him for a moment, then began to try to flap her wings. He was right. It didn't take much effort before they were both being bounced off of the ground. It was incredible. Once he was off of her enough, she rolled away and was free.

"Not bad for a fae. Maybe Quyen is right about you." He dusted himself off and gave her a pat on the back.

Brynn smiled.

"Let's give this another go. This time, use

your wings to your advantage."

"What do you mean?"

"Those things aren't just for show, Brynn. If I try to grab you, block me with them. You can try to flap them hard one time and the force can knock people away. Use your assets."

"How do you know all of this?"

"I don't know. Just a feeling, I guess. It will work. I promise."

Brynn nodded. As soon as Gideon looked ready, she charged him. She caught hm off guard, but damn he was strong. It was like slamming into a brick wall.

Gideon laughed at her attempt, and it made her see red. H tried to grab her again, but she took his advice and spread out her wings. It worked. He couldn't get through. She was surprised.

"I told you it would work." Gideon shouted with a smirk.

She gave her wings one hard flap and sent

him flying back a few feet. This was awesome.

For a moment, she felt like maybe she *could* be the girl in the prophecy. She waved it out of her mind. She needed a water break and she wanted to take a peek at Max. She could see him in the corner of the yard with Quyen. They were both fighting so hard, and he was so fast. It was remarkable.

She stood in quiet contemplation as she watched him move so effortlessly. He was beautiful. She wished that she could keep up with him.

"Their speed is impressive to watch, isn't it?"

She turned to see Gideon watching alongside her and she smiled slightly. She didn't want to tell him how jealous of Quyen she was right now. She supposed it was all over her face anyway. She tried to brush it off.

"Do you want to practice some more?"

"Actually, I'd really like to pick your brain a bit. I think it would be helpful. Truth be told, I don't know a ton about fairies... mostly just hate fueled rumors that I have heard over the years."

They found a secluded spot in the yard and sat down to talk. They were supposed to be fighting, but this seemed important too. If he was willing to go into battle with fairies, he should at least know what he was getting into.

"I think you are the only mystica that spends time in the human world. How do people not notice how different you are?"

"We have really good concealing spells. We hide our wings, soften our pointy ears, and majorly dull our shimmer. People know that we are different, but we aren't different enough for them to ask too many questions. When people wanted me to hang out after school and I couldn't, I just said that I had to go home every day to practice my faith. They started assuming we are just a weird religious cult. It made them nervous enough to stop asking."

"Don't take this personally, but I think that is just not worth the risk. Being around humans so often can just raise so many questions."

"I can understand that. I know we are one

of the only groups that does it. I suppose it has its pros and cons."

"How do you get away with saying you are in a religious cult? You guys can't lie, right?"

"That's true we cannot. It wasn't a lie, though. I did go home and practice my spells and whatnot. I never said I was in a cult. I just didn't correct their assumptions. There are many ways to get around the truth without telling a lie. You can evade, redirect, avoid... wording is everything. I know it sounds manipulative, but so is lying and everyone else does that."

Gideon gave quite a hearty laugh.

"I suppose you are right. I don't know if I would act any differently if I were in your shoes. I think there is probably a lot that we could learn from each other. Did you know that most mystica get along with each other? Fairies have always been the main exception. Everyone else has found some sort of a way to coexist. We clash from time to time, of course, but we make it work."

"Max is the first that I have known. Being a fairy, I was always too sheltered from the mystica world to get to know anyone. He was a human when we met... long story. Being with him has made me so angry that we have been kept away from others. There is nothing evil about him. He is a person just like me. The elders' way of thinking is so incredibly flawed. It only holds us back."

"I bet you would be surprised to know that your family and mine have a history that goes very far back. One that doesn't only include taking a family member hostage at that. Truth be told I don't know a ton of details. I never asked about the story. I was a bit disturbed by it, actually. Mostly because I hated fairies for what they had done to my uncle. Now that I have met you, I wish that I had asked about it. You have definitely changed my mind about your kind. From what I do know of the details, it was quite a love story."

"A love story? How long ago was that?"

"From what I understand, it was a generation or two before our grandparents. I'm not the best at following my genealogy. I think it involved one of my uncles. His name was Adam, I believe. I'm not sure how his wife was related to you."

"His wife? Do you know what her name was?"

"Hmm." He pondered for a moment. "Maybe Marie or Maria. Something like that, I think. Don't quote me on it, though. I could be way off."

"That's crazy. After all of this craziness is behind us, I will have to see what kind of info I can dig up."

"You'll have to let me know what you come across."

Brynn was very shocked to hear Gideon's revelation, but it brought her much happiness. Until now, she had lived a life of such isolation. If they could make it through this upcoming battle, she would have so many people in her life to love. What a change it would be.

The two of them sat together in the yard and carried on with their chat while the others continued to practice for battle. They didn't speak much more about the love story, but mostly about their differences. One by one, everyone began to wind down and tire out from this faux battle.

Vincent called for everyone's attention. You could see the pride on his face. He was clearly pleased with everyone's hard work and dedication thus far. He should be, too. Everyone was putting aside their differences and personal schedules to come together as a unit. It might not be a big deal for the other mystica, but it certainly was for the fairies.

"Now that we are all a bit weary from fighting, why don't we adjourn into the house to discuss finishing touches on our tactical plan. There are still many decisions to be made."

Gideon stood up, grabbed Brynn's hands, and pulled her up.

"I know he's a vampire, but do you think your dad is gonna give us a lunch break?"

"I wouldn't hold my breath." Brynn laughed and followed the rest of the crowd inside.

"We have some food in the oven as well. I know everyone could use a bit to eat.

Preparations can be depleting."

Brynn just started laughing. What were the odds of that timing?

After everyone grabbed a plate of food and some much-needed water, Vincent got right down to brass tacks. There wasn't much time to eat when planning a war. If they expected to make it out alive, they had to be prepared.

He went over every aspect of battle. From opening the portal and crossing over, to who would attack and cast first, he left no stone unturned, even those that had already been turned once or twice. Their execution had to be perfect. The people they were up against were much older than most of them and definitely more seasoned. They would be outnumbered as well.

Once he was finished reviewing the plans, he called on each person individually to ensure they were aware of and comfortable with their role in the battle. To Brynn, it felt a lot like she was back at school. The professor teaching the lesson to the class, then calling on them to make sure they were listening. And people thought it was stupid for fairies to go to public school. It was obviously teaching her skills, she laughed to herself as she had the thought.

"I do have one more request and I realize it might be a bit strange and uncomfortable for some of you." Vincent began, catching everyone's attention. "I would like you all to start staying here at our home until the battle is over. The day is near, and we don't want to take any chances. We need to be together when it is time to open the portal. This will also offer you protection. We do not know if the court has been watching us or not. If they have, then each of you could be a target. As it stands, they cannot get through the wards that we currently have up. If they are watching us, though, they have seen all of you coming and going. I can't force you to stay, but I do hope that you see why it is important. Trust me, a houseful of people doesn't excite me either. I've never been a slumber party kind of guy. Go and tie up loose ends if you have them and come back as soon as you can. Is there anything anyone would like to add?"

Bruce stood up next to Madeleine and cleared his throat.

"As promised, I have been keeping a close eye on the other plane. I am unsure if they know what we are planning here, but there has been much activity as of late. It would seem that they are on high alert. Although a definite inconvenience, I do agree with Vincent. We are all best suited to stay here for now." He sat back down and whispered something to Madeleine.

Brynn was surprised that no one put up a fight about staying at her house. Everyone understood why it was important. She was still having a challenging time grasping the concept of these people wanting to help her and her family, but it was definitely something that she could get used to. Almost everyone left, but with a promise of coming back before nightfall. Madeleine cast some sort of spell on each of them before they left, but she wasn't sure what kind it was. She had bigger things on her mind.

Bruce said the time to go to the other plane was quickly approaching. That meant it was almost time for her to assume this leadership role that she was still more than uncertain about. Just the thought of it made her a bit queasy.

"So, you and the bear seemed to be getting close earlier. That something I should be worried about?"

Max's question annoyed her. They were preparing for a fight, was he seriously being jealous right now?

"Check your tone, Max. I don't appreciate it. For your information, we were discussing many things, including our family histories. The more we know about each other, the better advantage we have." Her facial expression was enough to tell Max that he was out of line. He apologized, but still couldn't shake the feeling that there was something deeper there. Perhaps he was just being paranoid. They were all under so much stress and emotions were beginning to run high. Not to mention the fact that he was still figuring out how to be a vampire. All he could do was trust Brynn. He didn't need clouded judgement right now, anyway. He had to focus on the fight. So, he told her he was sorry once more and dropped the subject.

They could hear people talking in the kitchen. Brynn was hungry and that was not helping her mood at all. She should have eaten when everyone else did, but she was too nervous. So, they got up to join them.

"Where is dad?" Fiona asked as Max and Brynn entered the room.

"He went out to get a few cots and air mattresses for our friends. They should be coming back soon, and he wanted them to be as comfortable as possible." Shyan explained. "Brynn, you should hurry up and eat before this place is packed with people. Max, Vincent left some blood for you."

Everyone sat in the kitchen as Brynn and Max consumed their dinner in silence. They all had the same thing on their minds, but they were tired of talking about it. It was better to have their meal in peace. There would be a lot more talking over the next few days. For now, they ate and retired to their rooms before their company arrived.

"Sleep well. It will be sensory overload soon." Max kissed Brynn on the top of her head before retiring to his room.

SIXTEEN

When Brynn finally opened her eyes, she realized she was being shaken awake. How long had she been asleep? She couldn't tell.

"Brynn! Wake up! Bruce is downstairs waking everyone up. Something is wrong."

Brynn flew out of bed and followed her sister to the living room where everyone else was. Bruce looked rough and on edge, his hair aloof and eyes glassy, waiting for everyone to pile in so he could make some sort of announcement.

"Now that you are all here, I will speak. I am sorry for startling and waking you all, but I was just checking in on the other plane. This is usually the quietest time to visit, but tonight there was much activity afoot. They are organizing quickly. I think we need to make our move now. They won't be expecting us in the dead of night. We must move with haste and attack them before they hit us."

No one said a word, but rather sat in surprised silence for a moment. This was it. Shock. It felt surreal, especially to Brynn. She definitely thought that they had a few more days before this would come to a head. She wasn't ready for this. Her heart began to race, and she was pretty sure there wasn't a millimeter of space on her body that wasn't covered with sweat. Could anyone see how clammy her entire being had just become? She hoped not. This was really it.

One by one, everyone in the house began to get dressed in their fighting attire. No one questioned Bruce. He was the only one that had any connection to the other plane. Everyone one of them trusted him completely. Once they were all ready, they made their way to the basement. After everyone filed in and shut the door behind them, Bruce and Drake began to open the portal.

It was unlike anything that Brynn had imagined. In her mind she had pictured a giant black hole. This portal looked like a galaxy. It had swirls of purple, black and blue. It was moving in a clockwise motion, and she could swear it was filled with thousands of tiny stars.

They were all pretty tired from being suddenly awakened. Some of them had just fallen asleep when Bruce arrived. Madeleine cast a few regenerating spells on everyone to perk them up. Brynn immediately felt awake, powerful, and ready to fight. Not only was she awake, but she could feel adrenaline surging through her. She didn't know what spells had been cast, but they seemed incredibly powerful.

"Once we go through, there is no coming back until this is over. Does everyone know what their responsibility is in this fight?" You could hear the eagerness and vengeance in Vincent's voice. Everyone nodded, but no one said a word. "Okay, let's go!"

They went through the portal in the order they would stand before the court. First, the people that would no doubt be expected – Vincent, Shyan, Brynn, Fiona, and Drake. They were the known traitors of the realm. Max, Madeleine, Gautier, and Bruce followed closely behind them. The rest of the crew came in two shifts. First came the shifters, then the wolves. The mystica in the back remained out of sight. They needed to be a surprise. Bruce stayed close to the portal once they were all on the other side.

Seeing the other plane hit everyone hard. There was something off about it. The colors were all a bit hazy and dull, and it was almost as if they were moving while standing still.

"What's wrong with this place?" Fiona asked timidly, trying to regain her balance. She felt like she was inside of an accordion.

"They were expecting us. Madeleine, break the spell! Fiona and Drake, protection spells now!" Shyan shouted and everyone got into position immediately. Brynn was trying not to panic.

Madeleine began casting dispel while Fiona and Drake bumped up everyone's attributes by casting protect, shell, bravery, and focus. Bruce stayed close to the portal, but Brynn could hear him muttering to himself. She knew he must have been conjuring up some sort of dark magic. That is what warlocks were best at. He no doubt had some spectacular things up his sleeve.

"Show yourselves!" Madeleine demanded once she was finished casting.

Slowly colors began to return to their normal saturation, and everyone stopped feeling seasick. Once the feeling passed, however, the court members began to present themselves. There were a lot of them. More than Brynn had actually been envisioning while she was preparing. The nausea was quickly replaced with dread for most of them.

"You still haven't learned your lesson, have you Vincent?" One of the elder court members began. "We set you up to become a vampire and you are still trying to be a fairy. You are pathetic."

That was all that Vincent needed to hear. Their baiting worked. He lunged at the nearest fairy and ripped him to shreds in one swift move. Brynn couldn't tell if the look on the fairies' faces was surprise or just plain horror. What did they expect? And just like that, the battle had begun.

Madeleine charged full speed toward the court members, sword swinging as soon as she got close. Brynn watched in awe for a moment. She was faster than any fairy she had seen before. It had to be the adrenaline, but it was something to be admired. This was no time to stand and observe, though. Max, Brynn, and Gautier followed suit and began attacking the court members.

The vampires did what they did best and began to bite, shred, and rip apart the court just as Vincent had begun moments before. Brynn didn't have that speed and strength to her advantage, but she was holding her own with her own mix of martial arts and stabbing. While her enemies were no doubt excellent casters, she was pleased to find that fighting was not one of their strengths. They were much easier to dominate than she had expected them to be. She took Gideon's advice and used her wings to her advantage as much as she could. She could feel spells being cast on her, but their effects were short lived. Fiona must have been doing a good job taking care of all of them.

How were they able to cast harmful spells on her? She should be immune from such attacks. Fairies weren't supposed to be able to do that to each other. She wanted to ask, but she didn't want to give any weaknesses away. For all the court members knew, they could have been expecting the spell attacks. It was never even mentioned in their planning. It was always assumed that aside from healing and positive spells, it would be a physical battle. She would have to continue to fight as if she were not caught off guard.

She could see the shifters out of the corner of her eye as they approached the battlefield. All three of them were already in their animal forms. She was astounded at the size of them. Gideon was massive. The ground shook with each step that he and Raef took. The fairies didn't stand a chance against them, and they knew it. They immediately changed their strategies and began to feverishly cast spells. It was hard for Fiona and Drake to keep up with.

The wolves must have seen their friends starting to struggle, because she saw them leap out from the invisibility shield that they were shrouded by. The shock the court felt when they saw the wolves was visible. Just like a pack of wild dogs, they began tearing the fairy adversaries to shreds. It looked like a scene straight out of a horror movie. There were bits of clothing and fairy flying through the air. If it weren't for the adrenaline pumping through everyone's veins, some of them might have been a bit squeamish.

The court double backed in an attempt to get some space in between them and their attackers. Once they were able to get that, the wounded began to heal at an alarming rate. In the blink of an eye, they were rebuffed and ready to fight again. Their casting seemed to be even stronger and much, much faster.

As everyone was trying to close the gap in between them, Drake was suddenly lifted into the air. Everyone turned to look as he was slammed down into the ground. Brynn had never seen anything like it. Once again, he was picked up and slammed down, again and again. After the last drop to the ground, he didn't move. They could all see him lying there on the ground, completely motionless. Fiona cried out a terribly heartbreaking sound. She wanted to run to him and gather him in her arms, but she knew that she had a job to do. If she abandoned her duties, it could lead to more of the people that she loved getting hurt.

"Focus on the others Fiona. I will help him." Bruce said in a commanding, yet somber tone. Everyone knew the emotional tug-of-war that she was feeling.

She did just as Bruce instructed and tried to protect everyone as best she could. She had barely gotten her first spell out before she heard a yelp. There was too much activity around for her to see who had gotten hurt. A bear would have growled. It had to have been Quyen or one of the wolves. There was no real way of knowing yet.

"Madeleine! I need help! I can't cast fast enough." Fiona cried out to her aunt. With Drake being down, she couldn't handle it without him. It was just too much. She could see Madeleine back away from the action. She breathed a sigh of relief. Thank God she wasn't going to be on her own. There was no way that one person would be enough to keep everyone healed. There were fairy bodies lying all around them, but they were still outnumbered.

Another yelp.

This time, all of the wolves started to howl. It was like there was a full moon or something. The first animal howl must have been from Quyen because there were no howls afterward. Why did it have to be someone else that she had gotten somewhat close to? She couldn't take much more of this. She wanted to rush in and seek her out to help, but she knew that she couldn't do that. She couldn't help Quyen right now just like there wasn't shit that she could do for Drake.

"Bruce! Quyen is hurt, but I don't see her!"

He didn't reply, but she hoped that would be enough to get him on the job. It would take some of his focus off of Drake, but she trusted

Bruce. Warlocks were as powerful as they came. If anybody were a savior to the wounded, it would be him.

He didn't come to her aide, though. Instead, she saw him dig through his pocket and pull out a small vial of pink liquid.

"Maddie. It's time for Plan B." He said in a stern, yet urgent voice and Madeleine made her way to his side.

"Let's end these SOBs." He said with a sadistic smile and Madeleine began to cast some sort of spell.

No one else seemed to notice what was going on other than Fiona. They were all continuing to fight. She knew that she should be focusing on her job, but she couldn't tear her eyes away from what was unfolding behind her. What were they doing?

Madeleine was still casting when Bruce opened up the vial of liquid and poured it in his hands. He began slowly rubbing them together, watching Madeleine intently. Once she was finished casting, he opened up his hands like a book and presented them to her. She blew on them as hard as she could. What was once potion turned into a giant pink missile of sorts and jumped from Bruce's hands into the air. Fiona watched as it seemed to target each member of the court as it launched their way.

The court didn't have time to react to this unexpected assault. The pink arsenal rained down on them, crippling everyone it touched. It didn't kill anyone, but once people were over the shock of an attack they weren't told about during all of the previous planning, it was enough to finish the job. They pounced on the weakened court members and began to take them out. They weren't able to get them all, unfortunately. There were a handful of the strongest court members that were able to make an escape. You could tell that they had planned an escape in case of an overwhelming attack of sorts. It was fine. What mattered was that they eliminated the majority of them.

As soon as the court was gone, the prisoners began appearing all over the plane. They were all in cages of sorts and in various stages of abuse and malnourishment. There must have been a concealment spell that shattered once the court was gone. It was clear that their lives had been treated with utter disregard. Everyone was shocked and choked up.

Bruce cast a spell to release them from their hell.

Animals immediately began running and jumping about, but it took the rest of the prisoners a little longer to get their bearings. Brynn was excited to see the cat she so badly wanted to keep from the garden run and jump in her arms. That cat had been a symbol of hope for her when she created it. Now it was a success. This time she was keeping it.

As soon as the prisoners began moving about and they were certain there were no court members left, Fiona ran to Drake. Her scream told them everything that they needed to know. Brynn was crushed. Her sister went out of her way to make sure she could be with Max. She knew how important love was. Now the court had ripped that away from her. Her sobs could be heard over the conversations being had and Shyan made a move to go try to comfort her daughter as best she could.

Brynn suddenly remembered that more people had been injured. Quyen. She pushed through the people that were surrounding her to see if she could see the shifters. She spotted them just as Raef was picking her up.

"Is she..." she couldn't say the words.

"She's alive." Gideon said, barely holding it together,

"Get her back to my place. Bruce and Brynn, go with them." Vincent said with his constantly authoritative voice.

Max headed toward Brynn and was stopped when Vincent put a hand on his shoulder.

"I need you to stay with me." he said, looking Max firmly in the eye.

"What if Brynn needs me? I can't feel her energy if we are in separate planes."

"You would be going for the wrong reasons. I can feel what you feel, Maximillian. Jealousy is an ugly attribute to exhibit. Don't let it cloud your judgement. I need you here."

"Why did you send her back with them anyway?"

"Bruce is the only one who can heal Quyen. Her injuries are dire, and he is an enormously powerful warlock. He is the only one we have that even has a chance. Brynn has the biggest heart of anyone I know. It just comes natural for her. She is the right person to send for support. It isn't overly complicated son."

Max looked away, feeling ashamed that Vincent knew exactly what his motives were. What was he supposed to do though? Brynn could deny it all she wanted, but there was a spark between her and that damned bear. He certainly didn't want them spending any time alone together. If only he could feel her on the home plane.

SEVENTEEN

Brynn was horrified at what she was seeing back at home. She would feel bad about it later, but she wasn't even thinking of Max now. Quyen's limp body had been placed on the couch and Bruce was pulling several items out of a bag that he had left behind in the house. She had no idea what he was up to.

The guys probably knew more about the spell he was going to cast than she did. Warlock spells were completely different than fairy spells. Their magic was drawn from unusual places. Understanding them was- like trying to read a book written in a different language. It was useless to even try.

She looked at both of them as they watched him try to heal their cousin. Raef was stone-faced. He wasn't even blinking. Gideon on the other hand looked like he might vomit. He looked up with bloodshot eyes and caught her eye.

"I'm so sorry." She half whispered; half mouthed in his direction. He walked over to her and collapsed into her arms. Her heart began to break and race at the same time. For the first time since she crossed back over, she thought of Max. She was thankful that he was too far away to feel what she was feeling. He wouldn't understand and she didn't know how to explain it.

They held each other and watched as Bruce began to cast some sort of spell that looked very powerful on Quyen. Brynn rubbed Gideon's back as he rested his head on her shoulder. Not only did it feel nice to have a friend that knew everything about what she was, but it was nice to feel like she could be there for them. It wasn't often that someone looked to her for help or comfort. At least not until recently.

"All we can do now is wait. I think she will pull through. She is an extraordinarily strong girl." Bruce said as he walked away from Quyen. "I am going to stay near the portal. The others should be back soon, and I will need to close it behind them. I will return if you need me."

"I'm gonna go get some fresh air while the wards are still up and before people come back and start asking questions. I'm not ready to talk about this yet." Raef said, startling Brynn. He had been sitting so quietly behind her that she had forgotten he was there for a moment.

"Do you want to go with him before everyone else comes home? I can watch over Quyen." Brynn offered, still rubbing Gideon's back and not even realizing it.

"No, I'd rather stay here with you. Raef

can be hard to talk to. You are very comforting to be around and it's not just because of the killer back rub." He winked at her, and she became acutely aware of their contact. "Ever since we met each other, you've been very easy to talk to and I am very relaxed around you. There is just something about you… it's welcoming."

As Brynn smiled at the nice compliment she had just been paid, Gideon turned his head and kissed her. She didn't stop him. Her hand was already on his back, and she continued to kiss him. He put his massive hand on the side of her face. She savored the feel of his soft, warm lips as he pulled her in closer to him. The air around them felt electric. Her skin tingled beneath his touch.

He slowly slipped his hand underneath her shirt, keeping it on the small of her back. The smell of cinnamon flooded her nose and unlike the last time she was close enough to notice it, she couldn't get enough. She slid her hand down his chest, noticing just how defined his abs were. She traced them with her fingers before coming to a rest at the top of his waistband. Her heart was beating wildly. Before she got more carried away than she already was, she pulled away.

"I'm so sorry. I shouldn't have." Gideon said quickly.

He knew he crossed the line, but something about Brynn had been drawing him in since the first day he saw her. Even after he went home that day, she was all that he could think about. He didn't know why. He barely even knew her. She had begun taking up permanent residence in his mind, though.

"I just... It's... I mean... It's Max." she was so flustered. "See, he's had my blood. I mean, that's not the only thing about him, but yeah."

"So, he can tell what you are feeling. I understand. I'm not trying to come in between anything you have going on in your life, Brynn. I'm not going to lie and say that I don't have feelings for you, because I do. They were instant. I am fine being your friend, though, as long as you will still have me."

"Of course, I will. Gideon, my feelings have not been completely innocent either, but I can't let myself be that type of person. Your friendship has already meant a lot to me, and I will be damned if a kiss is gonna end it. I just don't know how to keep Max from knowing what is going on inside my head. Being connected like that can be nice, but it can also be a big hinderance." They both laughed.

"Just remember, you can always put a block in your mind to keep prying eyes out. It would suck not having any privacy."

She wanted to gush about how much she hated having all of her thoughts and feelings on display. How embarrassing it was to not have a single moment where she wasn't afraid to have a normal teenage girl thought or desire. She didn't want to put that on him, though.

"No actually, I didn't know that. Do I do it to myself or does someone do it for me?"

Gideon laughed, starting to realize how little Brynn actually knew.

"Either way should work. Since you are a fairy, you should be able to block yourself. Someone like me would need to seek out a fairy or warlock for help with it. I don't know the spells or anything, but from what I understand, you just think about what you want to block out and will it to be so. Or something like that, at least."

"That is not nearly detailed enough, but what the hell. I guess I'll try." She teased as she closed her eyes to focus. Who knew if this would work or not? With everything going on, though, she could really use a little more privacy than she had been getting.

She tried to focus on a few specific things that she wanted Max to not know about. She didn't want to block everything. That would be a major red flag. It would only make things worse.

Ugh, she felt like a sleaze ball right now for even doing this. It would be better this way. Things were so turbulent and the last thing she needed was for Max to lose his temper.

Only time would tell if she did it right or not. No need to dwell on it any longer, so she changed the subject.

"What do you think they are doing on the other plane?"

"It's hard to say. There is probably so

much to do. I'm sure your dad wants to try to speak to prisoners if they are willing. They will have a lot of information. Hopefully..."

They sat there watching Quyen, reliving the battle they had just been through.

EIGHTEEN

Prisoners were wandering around the plane. Some confused, some just looking for a way out. Vincent made eye contact with one of them and headed his way.

"How long have you been here, sir?"

"It's hard to say. It is easy to lose track of time here. It passes faster than you'd expect."

"What year did you arrive?"

"2015. What year is it now?"

"2022." Vincent said somberly.

"Seven years... oh what I will have missed. My loved ones left to wonder what became of me."

"I'm sure they have been looking for you. Go now. Find your family. Come find me if you need help."

"Thank you for what you all have done for me... for all of us. I didn't think I would ever get to leave this horrible place."

"Happy to have a hand to lend." Vincent had so many things he wanted to ask. This was not the time for any of that.

"Ok everybody, I know saying that you are anxious to get home is a severe understatement. I don't want to keep you here. I do have a great many questions for all of you. The more information we get, the better off we will be. As you are probably aware, we were not able to kill all of the court members responsible for this. We want to find those that got away. They do not get a chance to do this again. We also need to find out what they were doing here and why they were doing it. I ask that you all please contact me as soon as you possibly can. Your family, our allies, who fought with us know where to find me. I am not going to track you down. You have suffered enough. I just ask that you please consider my request and understand how much it can help."

One by one each mystica family left with their newly reunited loved one with a promise of contact. Vincent had no reason to doubt them. Without him and his family they would still be held captive. They would want to help.

"That just leaves what to do with all of these animals I suppose." Vincent said, looking around at all of the furry creatures roaming about.

"They will be fine to stay here for a bit. I can cast a spell to get them fed for today at least. There is a lake to the west with plenty of water for them to drink. This way we can get home and figure it out there." Madeleine suggested. Once she saw Vincent nod, she began casting.

It didn't take her long. When she was finished, he bent over and picked up Brynn's cat. The hardest part of this now was going to be Fiona. She was still at Drake's side sobbing. Shyan was stroking her hair like she used to do when Fiona was little. He made his way over to them.

"I am going to bring Drake home, sweetheart. Can you carry this cat back for me please?'

"Vincent, I don't think…" Shyan began to suggest that he give the cat to someone else, but Fiona got up and grabbed it from his arms. She needed as much comfort as she could get right now. Shyan stood up, put her arm around Fiona and led her to the portal. She didn't want her to see Vincent pick up Drake. It was hard enough to see him on the ground. It would be even worse to see his lifeless body being toted around.

Once everyone else was away from the realm, Vincent knelt down beside Drake. He left out a deep sigh. This poor boy loved Fiona enough to put his life on the line. It was ripping him apart that it had come to this. He didn't wish it on any of them, but why did it have to be this boy?

"I'm sorry, Drake. You were brave. You were worthy of my daughter. I will make sure we keep your memory alive. Thank you for the sacrifice that you have made for us."

He knew that Drake couldn't hear his words, but he needed to say them anyway. He gently picked him up off the ground and cradled him in his arms. As he slowly walked to the portal, he looked around them. So many lives were saved today, but this loss would be felt deeply. He hoped when he crossed back over, people would have made themselves scarce. Especially Fiona. That was unlikely, though. He took a step through the portal and was back in his room in a flash.

Bruce was standing by the portal when Vincent crossed through the other side with Drake. He quickly sealed it off to ensure that no unwanted visitors tried to come through behind them. His brow furrowed when he saw Drake in Vincent's arms.

"Let me try to do something for him." he said to Vincent, with a tone that suggested he was trying to be confident but knew that it was misplaced.

"It would be of no use, I am afraid. We must lay him to rest."

Fiona began to sob again as she heard the words her father spoke. She had been there waiting, just as Vincent feared. She put the cat down on the floor and it scampered up the stairs presumably to find Brynn. Fiona followed quickly behind the cat. Seeing Drake's body was too much. She needed her sister now more than ever. If anyone could comfort her, it would be Brynn. They may not have been close in the past, but their bond had quickly become strong. She could help Fiona overcome this.

Brynn heard commotion coming from the basement and knew that everyone must be back. She started to put some more space in between herself and Gideon, but Max was there much too quickly for her to have the chance. Now was not the time for his jealousy. People were grieving. People were injured. People were dead. She was going to tell him to lay off, but she could hear Fiona coming and her heart instantly began to break. Her sobs were already uncontrollable.

"He's dead." Fiona said as soon as she saw Brynn's face. She collapsed into her arms. "He risked it all for us. This is my fault." She continued to sob hard into Brynn's chest. She didn't know what to do for Fiona. How do you comfort someone who has just lost the love of their life? How do you make them see that it is not their fault? She did the only thing that she knew to do and that was to stay there with her. She hugged her and rubbed her back.

Pretty soon Bruce slipped into the room. When Brynn noticed him, he put his finger to his lips and made a motion for her to stay silent. He quietly cast a spell and Fiona quickly fell asleep.

"That will ease her temporarily. She will not wake until tomorrow unless you want her to. She was not doing anyone any good in the state she was in. She needs rest."

Brynn thanked him and Max picked Fiona up and carried her to her bed. Brynn decided to go with him to make sure her sister was properly tucked in. She looked so peaceful under Bruce's spell. Once she awoke, though, she would begin torturing herself once again.

"Are you okay?" Max asked Brynn softly as she rubbed Fiona's face. Her poor baby sister.

"Fine, just stressed and overwhelmed. Sad. I don't know how I am going to be able to help her." She hadn't even begun to think about the fairies that died today by her hand. That would surely hit her later.

"How is Quyen?"

"She should pull through, thanks to Bruce. He is really amazing."

"So are you." He was trying hard to not be a jealous asshole, but he meant what he said. So many people were freed today because of her.

Brynn was too tired to acknowledge the compliment.

"I hear more voices. We should head back."

Max nodded and followed Brynn back into the living room. The rest of the family had finally made their way back into the main part of the house. They were all sitting down, exhausted. It sounded like they were discussing the funeral arrangements for Drake. They were planning on having it tomorrow. Fiona would not be ready for that when she woke up. Poor Fiona. They would just let her sleep until then. After the funeral is finalized, the next topic to discuss was what to do about Quyen.

"Quyen is in an extremely fragile state right now. I do not think that she should be moved until she is awake and stable." Bruce said.

"She is welcome to stay here indefinitely. That goes for you boys as well." Vincent was happy to oblige.

Raef and Gideon agreed that that was the best decision to be made. They did not want to leave their cousin. Brynn could feel Max roll his eyes. Was it just jealousy or did he feel threatened by Gideon? Whatever it was, she needed him to get over it ASAP. She had far too much on her plate to deal with these foolish things.

Had she made a mistake by taking things too far with Gideon? Absolutely. Did she have a lot of feelings that she didn't know how to deal with right now because of him? You bet. The mind block seemed to be working as far as she could tell. That would buy her some time to figure things out at least. Why did things have to be so complicated?

NINETEEN

They let Fiona sleep for most of the day. They woke her only early enough to let her know about the funeral and give her time to process it. They had to wait for the moonlight to shine to begin the ceremony, so Fiona stayed in her room until then. When it was time to start, Brynn went to Fiona's room to get her.

"Everyone is already outside, but I won't

let you do this by yourself." Brynn said as she grabbed her hand. "Be strong for him."

Fiona nodded and took a very deep breath. Her tears had stopped, but the sorrow in her eyes was deep. When the girls got outside, Madeleine began to talk.

"A lot of fairy folklore says that we do not die. I wish that were true. Drake didn't deserve to die. He fought bravely for us all and now we will bond him with this earth."

Fiona's eyes became misty as she looked at Drake. The fae traditions surrounding death were beautiful. Rather than following the human routine of putting the deceased into a box, fairies were wrapped in leaves and flowers and put directly into the ground. There were no chemicals or anything unnatural. This way their body became one with the earth that so graciously gave them their powers all of their years. They waited for the moonlight because that was when their magic was most powerful.

His body had already been wrapped up. The only part of him that you could see was his face. He looked so peaceful. They all began to sing, and a single tear fell from the corner of Fiona's eye. She had always loved the songs of their people. To her, they were so much more beautiful than the music humans listened to. If a passerby were to overhear the song, they would probably mistake it for some sort of Celtic lullaby. Science fiction fans would think it was the music of elves. It was truly a thing of beauty.

As she looked around, she noticed that the flowers began to open and close when the singing started. No one had seen anything like that before. Once it was over, they closed for good. She could feel Drake's presence.

Fiona approached Drake and touched his face softly before they lowered him into the ground.

"This isn't goodbye, because I know I will see you again. I love you Drakey." She tucked one last flower into his chest, kissed his forehead and stepped back. Vincent, Bruce, and Max lowered him into the ground. Everyone took handfuls of dirt and threw it into the hole he had been lowered into until it was filled. They continued to sing until the task was done. Shovels were never used in a fairy burial. Manmade tools were not necessary, as they wanted to be as connected to the earth as possible.

"This spot will forever be magical." Vincent said as the last handful of dirt came to rest on top of the mound. "The herbs and flowers that will grow around here will be special and powerful. They will be a lasting gift from Drake." He put his arm around Fiona and kissed the top of her head.

"I know this is hard sweetheart. You have a group of people here that love you and will get you through this dark time."

"I know." she said softly before heading back inside the house.

After a few minutes, Brynn walked into the house looking for Fiona. She found her sitting on her bed, hugging her legs.

"Mind if I come in?"

Fiona shook her head. Brynn walked in and shut the door behind her.

"I don't really know the right thing to say, Fi. I am so sorry about what happened to

Drake. But I do know that he loved you, and he didn't hesitate to risk everything to help you and our family."

"This hurts. I am so mad and so sad... What am I supposed to do?" She laid her head on Brynn's shoulder. Her shirt was soaked in tears in no time.

"I don't know. It sounds cliché, but Drake wouldn't want you to shut yourself away. Besides, it's gonna take both of us to get revenge." Brynn laid her head on Fiona's.

"I'd like that." Fiona smiled. "Will you stay with me tonight?"

"You bet. You gotta give me some of your pajamas, though, because I am not sleeping in jeans."

Fiona got some clothes out of her dresser and tossed them at Brynn. She changed and they both got into bed.

"Thanks, Brynn."

"You're welcome."

"I don't deserve you. I've been such a turd.

I wish things would've been different."

"They are now. That's all that matters."

"Good night."

"Good night, Fiona."

TWENTY

Life had just become so surreal within the past few days. A battle had been fought (and won), friendships were made, and a great fairy was laid to rest. Brynn wanted to relax but her head was filled with so many thoughts. What now? They needed to appoint a new court. What about the fairies at the compound? That relationship needed to be mended.

"You look like a fairy with a lot on her mind." Vincent said as he took a seat next to Brynn on the front porch. "I'm sure I can guess some of it. Your mother and Madeleine are on their way now to the compound to address the others. Hopefully, we will all be back on the same side... We can't start appointing a new court without them."

Brynn let out a big sigh.

"I feel so conflicted right now. I am completely overwhelmed, but also weirdly at peace."

"It is perfectly normal to be feeling overwhelmed right now, my girl. There is much left to do. As the one who paved the way for us, you are entitled to be involved in as much of the process as you would like. It is entirely up to you." Vincent stood up, patted Brynn on the top of the head and walked back into the house.

If she went all in on this process, guns blazing, it would mean two things. One, she would be spending a lot of time away from Max. That was a definite con. They were finally at a point in their lives where they could be together. It would also mean that she would have a chance to prove herself to the rest of the fairies that had always doubted her. That would be a definite pro. She had so much to think about and consider. Because this could potentially impact Max's life, it was only fair that she involved him in the decision-making process. She went inside to find him.

He was sitting inside the room that he had been sharing with Drake.

"Mind if I come in?" she asked as she knocked on the door frame.

"Of course not." He said, patting the bed. She took a seat beside him, and he put his arm around her. "It's weird being in here without him. I know we didn't share this room for long, but I had gotten used to him being here. I liked him."

She put her hand on his leg, comforting him without saying a word. This whole time, she was only thinking about how Drake's death affected the fairies. She never thought about the friendship that he and Max had formed in their time together at Vincent's. It made her feel a bit selfish.

"Ok, enough with the mushy stuff. What are you up to babe?"

For some reason, she became nervous now that it was actually time to talk to Max about life decisions. She needed his guidance, though so she had to go through with it.

"I wanted to talk about some future decisions I need to make. Your opinions would be very helpful. I honestly have no idea what to do. Dad told me that because of the role I played in this whole battle, that I can be in as much of the court appointing and rebuilding process as I want.

The upside is that I would finally get to prove myself to everyone that always doubted me. The downside is that it might take me away from you a lot more than we would like. I just don't know what to do here and I don't think I have a lot of time to decide."

Max sat there, thinking for a moment. Brynn just stared into his blazing vampire eyes the whole time. Those eyes. They were the first thing she noticed about Max. Now that he was a vampire, they were even more captivating. She could get lost looking into them.

"I think you should go for it Brynn. I will be with you every step of the way. It would be amazing to see you blossom even more than you already have." He touched her glistening face with his cold hand. "When I think I couldn't be more in awe of you, I am always surprised by what you unleash. There is no way that this would be any different."

She moved closer and kissed him. He put his other hand on her waist and pulled her into him.

"Your fangs haven't come out." Brynn said with genuine surprise. Normally when they got close, they popped out uncontrollably.

"I'm learning to control them."

"We will see about that." She said with a smile as she grabbed his neck and pulled him closer to her. He might have been cold, but they were creating enough heat that could convince anyone otherwise.

She pulled her face back and stared into his blazing eyes.

"I want you."

That was all it took to unleash his fangs. So much for self-control. Before she knew it, he had whisked her a mile away to their old park.

"What are we doing here?" she asked when he finally put her down.

She looked around, trying to figure out what he had up his sleeve. Not much was going on. There were two small families over by the playground equipment. She spotted two young people sitting on a blanket. It looked like they were there for a picnic but based on all of the kissing, they had forgotten about their lunch. Other than that, they had the park to themselves.

"I have a surprise for you. We have so much history here. I felt like this had kind of become our place. So, I made us our own hidden spot here. Your sister put some sort of glamour on it so no one else would see it. Now we have a secret hideaway."

Her heart burned at the thought of how much they meant to each other. All she could do was kiss him. He led her to their new hideaway, and she couldn't believe her eyes. Before she allowed herself to see past the glamour that Fiona had put on it, it just looked like a hill with some shrubs on it toward the back of the park near the tree line. Once they went inside, it looked like a studio apartment. There was furniture, a television and everything else that they could possibly need.

"I can't believe you did all of this, Max! This is incredible."

"I did it all for you, Brynn. I wanted to have somewhere to take you that we could be away from everyone. Somewhere to talk, somewhere to cry, somewhere to just be ourselves. I love you."

"I love you too." She said as Max bent down to kiss her.

He began walking her backward toward the couch until they made contact. They sat down, kissing the entire time. She had millions of butterflies in her stomach. Being with him this time was different than before. Without the fear of being caught, she had so many thoughts running through her brain.

Max had been the one talking about self-control earlier, but as his lips left hers and made their way down her neck, she knew that she had none.

She slid her fingers through the back of his hair and grabbed a handful. She knew that must have been a good move, because with lightning speed he took off his shirt and was right back to kissing her. She still wasn't used to his speed. She ran her hand down his chest and let it settle on his abs. They were ridiculously chiseled. She let her hand linger for a few moments.

"You know, it's not fair that I'm the only one with my shirt off here." He whispered in her ear. She giggled and they continued to play that game until there was a pile of clothing on the floor.

"We can slow down if you want to babe." Max said in between kisses.

She had been dreaming of sharing this moment with Max for such a long time. She was thinking about it even before they were spending much time together before he was a vampire. She was so happy in this moment.

"I love you Max. You are all that I want."
And after those words, her world went a bit
hazy.

In an instant, their bodies intertwined.
Max's fangs came out and for the first time, he
didn't seem to care. Brynn thought that it
looked so hot. Was he going to bite her? She
was so turned on that she probably wouldn't
even think twice about it. His icy touch was
all over her, but her body wasn't cold from it.

His vampire speed was a surprise. When
she had dreamed about this in the past, she
always pictured it at normal speed. This was a
little hard to keep up with. She liked trying to
though. He didn't say it out loud, but Max
liked it too.

They spent the next few hours just lying
on the couch, enjoying their time together.
They knew that no matter how much they
didn't want to, they needed to get back home.
She needed to check on Fiona as well as tell
her dad her decisions for the future.

"What are we gonna say if they ask where
we have been?" Max asked, suddenly seeming
shy.

"We have been talking at the park." Brynn laughed. "Carry me home?"

He was happy to oblige. Having a super-fast vampire boyfriend definitely had its perks. She hopped up on his shoulders and within a minute they were home. It was so much better than walking.

She came bouncing in the front door and was shocked to see that Quyen was awake. She immediately ran to her and hugged her.

"I am so happy to see you awake! How do you feel?"

"Pretty woozy, but so thankful to be alive. I will never be able to thank Bruce enough for what he did for me. And you for what you have done for all of us."

"I think you might be giving me too much credit, but I agree that Bruce is amazing. I know your cousins are happy to have you back."

"Don't sell yourself short, Brynn. You saved us. I knew that the prophecy was true."

"Since Quyen is awake now, we are going

to take her home. Thank you guys so much for all that you have done for her." Gideon said, intently staring at Brynn the entire time.

Did he know what just happened between her and Max? Could he sense it? She felt like it was written all over her face. She owed Gideon nothing. Why did she suddenly feel guilty?

"Come see me when you want to hear the rest of the prophecy, Brynn. I'd love to talk about it with you." Quyen said, putting her hand on Brynn's arm before they showed themselves out the door.

It gave Brynn a bit of a shiver. This whole time she assumed the prophecy was only about the battle. She thought that she knew all there was. She would definitely be taking Quyen up on her offer at some point. What else could there be?

"I'll go check on Fiona if you want to talk to your dad. I think he is in the basement." Max offered.

"Thanks. I really am eager to talk to him about things."

Based on Max's suggestion, Brynn checked the basement first. His vampire instincts were right, her dad was there.

"Hey sweetheart. What are you doing?"

"The shifters left."

"I figured they would be leaving soon. Quyen woke up about an hour ago. I didn't think they would stick around for very long once she came to."

"Are mom and Madeleine back yet? Have you heard anything about how things went at the compound?"

"They haven't made it back yet. I don't know how things are going, but if your mom was in danger I would sense it. They must be taking a while to sort things out I suppose."

"Well, I wanted to continue our conversation from this morning. I thought about it a lot and I talked to Max about it. I think that I would like to be fully involved with as much as I can."

Vincent smiled at Brynn. This was clearly the answer that he was hoping for.

"That makes me so happy. This is your destiny, Brynn. You and I are special. We were born to lead our kind. It is your time to shine and take the next generation of fairies into the future."

That thought filled Brynn with unmeasurable excitement and pride. For the first time, she felt like she was meant for something. Maybe this was what she was here for.

Vincent put his hand on Brynn's shoulder and looked down at his brave daughter. "You do realize this is just the beginning, right?"

TWENTY-ONE

It was late by the time Shyan and Madeleine made it home. Everyone was on pins and needles. There were so many things that could go wrong at the compound. For all any of them knew, fleeing court members could have gone there seeking refuge.

"Your mom and Madeleine are almost here." Vincent said eagerly as he stood up. He began pacing the living room.

They seemed to be in good spirits when they finally entered the house. Vincent rushed over to hug Shyan. It was so heartwarming seeing them have a second chance at love. That flame clearly hadn't burned out for either of them after all these years.

"I take it everything went well at the compound. I don't see any bloodstains or tattered clothes." He joked as he looked Shyan over.

"It went better than I think either of us thought it would. Maddie was the star of the show. Once everyone saw her and realized that they had all been fed a bullshit story all of these years, things really came together." Shyan smiled at her sister.

"We want to hear everything."

Shyan spent the next hour giving everyone the rundown on the conversation had at the compound.

"When we got there no one really knew what happened. The rumors had already begun circulating. Of course, many at the compound were close to some of the court members. People began to talk when the absence of those who died became apparent. As those that weren't killed made their way into hiding, a few got word to their families. I guess they didn't want them to worry when they didn't come home.

Really, they were just around long enough to try to paint us as the aggressors. Everyone probably would've bought it, especially if I hadn't shown up with Madeleine. Once she told them the truth about what had happened to her and Coulter, they were questioning everything.

We gathered everyone in the conference room. It was easier than repeating ourselves and playing the telephone game. The atrocities going on in the other realm was quite a shock to most of them."

"Once everyone was there, I recalled the last day that I saw any of them. I was walking to the park to meet Coulter. Before I made it there, someone came up behind me. He grabbed my arms and held them to my sides. I couldn't move. Someone else threw a cloth bag over my head. There was a sharp pain in my arm. Next thing I knew, I was waking up in the other realm. My arms and legs were tied to a chair. There must have been a tether spell cast on the rope because I could not break free.

I heard Coulter call my name. The court members drug him in front of me. I told him I was sorry. This was my fault. I was naïve. He managed to tell me he loved me before they started. As a group, they sliced through his skin like it was nothing. They tore him apart limb by limb. I will never be without the vision of the love of my life being tortured…bled to death. Only because he loved me.

They left me sitting there for hours just staring at what was left of Coulter. No one should have to see someone they love in a state such as that. It is a vision and memory that I will never be rid of. They laughed throughout everything. There was zero regard for his life." Madeleine choked back a tear. After all of these years, it was still hard for her to talk about Coulter.

"Everyone was shocked to her Maddie's story. Some were even crying. We also told them about Drake. It was just so heartbreaking. We told them about his bravery and the risk he took to save me. Who knows what would have happened if it weren't for him. His mother would like to visit soon to see where we laid him to rest."

Fiona began to silently cry. Max put his arm around her. She mouthed a "thank you" to him before resting her head on his shoulder.

"The fairies at the compound are now on our side. We have to be smart though, because the former court will want that alliance. That brings me to my proposition."

She hesitated, rubbing her hands together.

"I know how uncomfortable this could be, but I think it is our smartest move. We need to move to the compound. All of us. Without eyes and ears there, we could lose this fight."

"What about the vampires? We all know how they feel about them." Brynn piped up. To say she was concerned was an understatement. Wouldn't they just be walking into a trap?

"We spoke to them about that as well. They know that all other mystica interact and are friends with each other. It is time that fairies took part in that too. They will get used to it. Was it their favorite proposition to receive? No, it wasn't. It will be fine, though. I wouldn't suggest it if I thought otherwise."

Everyone looked at each other hesitantly. This could go great, or it could be a dumpster fire. Would the payout be worth the risk?

"Why don't we all take a day to think about it. There are so many things I miss about the compound, but I have many concerns about going back there as well. It's a big request. Let's take a day for it to sink in and give it some good thought." Brynn suggested.

She was just as nervous as anyone else. Her life at the compound had not been great. The thought of going back there, with two vampires that she loved at that, made her anxiety take center stage.

"I think that is a fair approach. You're right. It is a big request." Madeleine sighed. "It makes me nervous to be there too. When I was young, I thought it was such a magical place. After they turned on me, made my life hell... well, it doesn't exactly make me all warm and fuzzy inside. I do truly believe that it would be for the best, though."

TWENTY-TWO

"Could I have a word with you alone, Brynn?" Bruce asked in a hushed tone.

She nodded and followed Bruce down the hall into her bedroom. He carefully closed the door behind them and sat down on the edge of the bed, motioning for Brynn to join him.

She obliged.

"I know you have a lot of very important decisions to make. I have a suggestion that I hope you will take. Before you make any major decisions, you need to seek out Quyen. You need to know more of the prophecy before you continue. I believe the information could be imperative for your success."

"Is there really that much left in the prophecy that I don't know about it? Until Quyen mentioned it as she was leaving, I thought I knew everything. I figured it was simply that a fairy would rise up and start a new era."

"I do not know the full prophecy. It has been protected and passed down throughout many shifter generations. I am only privy to bits and pieces. Because of the little information I do know, I think it would suit you well to educate yourself a bit more. Having extra knowledge before making a major decision never hurt anyone. I want you to succeed. I would tell you myself, but it is not my place. Quyen should be the one to guide you through it."

"Okay, I will go speak with her. Now that so many eyes are on me, I am scared of making the wrong move. You are right. I need to seek out all of the information that I can. Besides, I am quite curious what else this story says about me." Brynn laughed and Bruce grinned at her. He was a bit odd, but his heart was good. He wanted nothing but good for Madeleine and the entire family. They were lucky to have him as an ally.

"Can I ask you something Bruce?"

"Of course, you can. I'm an open book."

"Well, I know you found Aunt Maddie in the other realm. It kind of sounds like you pushed everything aside and devoted your life to her. Why is that?"

"That is a very good question. Essentially, yes that is what I did. Don't get me wrong, I didn't stop seeking out information that led me there in the first place. I have continued that work. In fact, this battle with you and your family has been the pinnacle of it. As far as Madeleine goes... well, it is both simple and complicated at the same time. I think the easiest way I can explain it is when you know, you know.

I instantly felt pulled to her. When we

touched, it felt like fireworks. It felt as if the stars themselves were telling me that she was the one for me. My missing piece. I took her in and never looked back. She is the best part of me."

"Do you really think that there is a specific person for each of us?"

"Absolutely I do. I think it is predetermined. When we meet that person, the stars will make sure that we know."

"Thank you for everything Bruce. I'm really glad that you are here with us."

"As am I, young fairy queen. Now, I will let you get back to your own business. Thank you for hearing me out."

Brynn promised to call Quyen and set something up before the day was over, and she made good on her word as soon as he left her room. Quyen said that she would be available later in the evening, so Brynn was planning to go to her house. Max wouldn't be happy that she was going by herself, but if Bruce thought that she should go alone, that was what she would do. She needed to tell Max what her plans were ahead of time, though. She sent him a quick text asking him to come to her room. Hopefully, he wouldn't get the wrong idea about what she meant.

Considering the way he zipped into her room, he definitely thought she had something nefarious on her mind.

"Should I close the door?" Max asked eagerly.

Brynn felt bad for letting him down. Not only that, but she was about to deliver some news that he was not going to be happy about.

"No babe, that's not why I called you up her." She patted the bed next to where she was sitting, and he frowned a bit as he walked over to join her. "We need to talk about something."

"You realize conversations that start that way rarely end well, right?"

"It's nothing like that. I spoke to Bruce today and he thinks it would be a good idea for me to find out more of the prophecy before I make any major decisions. That has been on my mind too. So when he suggested it, I felt so validated. I am going to see Quyen this evening to talk and see what else I can learn."

"I notice you said I and not we... does that mean I'm not invited?"

Brynn sighed.

"It's not that I'm choosing to not invite you, but Bruce thinks it is a good idea for me to go alone. I can see why. I will probably approach it with more of an open mind if I am by myself. That isn't just about you either. I would probably feel influenced by anyone that was with me. You, dad, mom, Fiona... I know me."

"If we are being honest, Brynn, I don't like it. I'm sure you know that already. That's probably why you decided to tell me ahead of time, which I appreciate. It's not just about the bear either. This world isn't a safe place for you, babe. Especially now. I worry about you when you're not with me."

"I know things are extra dangerous right now. You will be able to feel me, though. If I am in danger, you will know it. With that lightning-fast speed, you would be there before anything bad could happen to me. I know you won't let anything happen to me."

"Never." He reached over and kissed her head.

"So, when are you leaving?"

"In a few hours. I don't expect to be there long. How much could there really be to this prophecy anyway?"

"It's hard to say. There already seems to be more than you expected to begin with. I will be happy for you to get more answers, though. I'm so proud of you for stepping up and taking charge of this new role that has been given to you. On the other hand, I feel kind of bad. I don't want you to be overwhelmed with decisions. In twenty years, I don't want you to look back on this time of your life and have regrets about choices you made because of the responsibility that you didn't ask for."

She wondered if anyone else had that thought. She had the same worries that Max did. That was something she wasn't letting herself think about. While she did not ask for this to be on her shoulders, she was going to embrace it. It was an amazing opportunity, not a curse. If this prophecy really was about her, she planned to live up to it.

TWENTY-THREE

The walk to Quyen's house took longer than Brynn expected. Max had offered to walk her there, but she didn't take him up on it. This would give her a chance to clear her head before she got there. She meant it when she told him that she knew she would feel influenced if anyone went with her. She wanted to focus on the prophecy and make the decisions she needed to make on her own. If things went badly, she wanted to have no one to blame but herself.

She saw Quyen's house up ahead in the distance. It was a beautiful light blue cottage in the woods. Lanterns and string lights lined the stone path to the front porch. It was dark outside, but she could still make out a bench off of the path. It was surrounded by bright flowers. There were so many flowers around the house that she was immediately consumed by the smell of gardenia and jasmine.

Before she could even finish knocking on the door, Gideon opened it and welcomed her with a smile. She hadn't even thought about him being here. Now she had butterflies in her stomach. Why?

"Good evening, princess. Quyen is super excited that you have come to learn more about the prophecy. It's all she's been talking about. She likes you."

"Thanks Gideon. I'm excited too. If she hadn't mentioned it when she left my house after the battle, I would have thought that there was no more to it. I'm very curious."

"I am too actually."

"You don't know the prophecy already?"

"Nope. As the oldest child of our generation, the secrets were entrusted to Quyen and Quyen only. I have only been able to learn more about it as you have. Until you know about it, I am in the dark. Trust me, it's something I have always been curious about."

Brynn was surprised. She assumed that they all knew more about the prophecy than she did. Gideon showed her to the living room and told her to have a seat as he went to find Quyen for her.

The suede couch was comfortable. It was soft and she sunk down in it the longer she sat there. This would be a good napping couch. All she needed was a blanket. Quyen greeted her with a big, genuine smile when she entered the room.

"Brynn! I am so happy to see you. I was hoping you would be by to see me sooner rather than later."

"How are you feeling? It looks like you have healed nicely. It's good to see you up and moving around so well."

"Yes, thanks to Bruce I am doing much better. I came really close to not being here anymore. To say I am grateful is quite an understatement.

That being said, I know you are eager to hear more of the prophecy. It comes with a bit of a disclaimer, though. You might not like some of the things that I tell you. I urge you to give those things some thought. Don't get mad or defensive. Don't just disagree and brush it off. Even if they seem unrealistic. The future has a funny way of knocking us off course."

"Yikes. That disclaimer makes me nervous right away. I trust you though. I promise I will give everything you tell me some thought. I won't act hastily. In the beginning, I know I brushed the prophecy off. That isn't something I can do anymore, and I know that. I will handle this better than I did initially."

With that, Quyen opened the notebook she was holding. It looked old and a bit tattered. Its leather cover was heavily creased.

There were several strings hanging out that she assumed used to be bookmarks. Just seeing it made her stomach swirl. The weight of everything got a little bit heavier.

"This prophecy has been handed down from generation to generation in my family. It is always given to the oldest child. When my mother gave it to me, she told me that I was to guard it with my life. If the fairy it speaks of wasn't of my time, I would pass it down to my oldest child when the time came. However, if that fairy did cross my path, it would be my responsibility to tell her of the prophecy. I would need to teach her, guide her, and swear my allegiance to her.

You *are* that fairy, Brynn. I will be in your corner and by your side for the rest of my days. I will never lead you astray. You can count on me."

Brynn swallowed the lump that had formed in her throat. The weight of Quyen's words hit her hard. She couldn't explain it, but she could feel it in her soul. For the first time since this all started, she did feel like the fairy in the prophecy.

"I cannot tell you everything at one time. You are supposed to receive this message in segments. That will allow you to absorb the information properly. I know after tonight you will want to know more... want to know everything. Trust me when I tell you that I cannot do that. When the time is right, I will tell you what is necessary. You won't have to come to me for more. I will come to you based on what events and decisions take place."

Brynn nodded. She knew Quyen was right. She would want to know every single detail before she went home tonight. That was going to be tough. It made sense though. How could she possibly remember everything if there was that much to tell? Should she have brought something to take notes with?

"As you already know, you have been awakened and led your people into the first battle for change. The fairies will be looking to you now for guidance. It's not just the fairies, though. The whole mystica world will need you. This prophecy is about you creating a new world. A world where we all coexist and work together in order to preserve what we are.

In the coming weeks, you will assemble a new court. You will need representatives on the court for fairies and the others. How that works is up to you. The details don't matter that much. You aren't supposed to do it alone, though. You are supposed to have a partner in this. He will stand for the other mystica as you do the fairies."

Quyen hesitated, almost as if she didn't want to or know how to say the next part. How bad could it be?

"Brynn, that partner for you is Gideon. He doesn't know this. As I heard him tell you earlier, he does not know anything about the prophecy until you do. Tonight will be the first that he hears of this. Look, I know there is something between the two of you. What that something is right now, I do not know. I also know that your relationship with Max will make this feel complicated for you. It is necessary, though. You must find a way to make it work."

"When you say partner, you just mean professionally right? I'm not expected to throw everything away and have some arranged marriage, right? Max is in this world now because of me. The thought of throwing that away... I can't do that. He deserves better than that."

"I am not telling you to do that. The prophecy speaks of you and Gideon leading all of us into a new era. It doesn't give me a detailed account of your love life. I would never suggest that you make rash decisions like that right now. The balance is delicate, and you need to keep it like that as much as you can. That being said, don't make any decisions you don't want to just for the sake of keeping the balance."

Brynn rubbed her eyes. It felt like Quyen was talking in riddles.

"There is not a lot more to tell you tonight. For now, you are to select and assemble the new court. Give it a new name. Pick your representatives. Find a way to form your partnership with Gideon. I will speak to him after you leave about his role in the prophecy. If you could wait until to tomorrow to peak of it, I would be appreciative."

"You have definitely given me a lot to think about. I will let it all sink in at home tonight. Honestly, it is a lot more to take in than I expected. I'm grateful that I'm not getting the whole prophecy tonight. And don't worry, I won't say anything to Gideon." Brynn laughed as she got up from her seat.

"You can do this Brynn. You were destined for greatness."

Quyen gave Brynn a hug before she turned to leave.

"I will call Gideon tomorrow and we can figure out where to go from here. Thank you for everything, Quyen. I'm glad that I have you with me for this. I don't have a huge group of friends, but I'm glad you're one of them."

As Brynn walked through the hallway leading to the door, Gideon stopped her.

"Would you like me to walk you home? It's gotten pretty late and dark outside." He offered as he opened the door for her.

"Thanks Gideon, but I'll be fine on my own. I have a lot to think about tonight and the walk home might be the only quiet time I get to think things over. Besides, I'm not afraid of the dark."

"I get it. It was good seeing you, Brynn. Don't be a stranger."

She smiled at his comment. Being a stranger wasn't even a possibility for them now. He would know soon enough. Hopefully, he would be an easy person to work with. A fleeting feeling of dread flushed through her.

How was she going to explain this plot twist to Max? He had been so temperamental lately. She felt like she was walking on eggshells at times. Quyen was right. This was delicate and she needed to work hard to keep the balance.

Maybe she would be lucky, and he would understand. This wasn't something that she had come up with on her own. She didn't seek this out. Any of it.

Thank God she came alone. She needed this time to think. There was so much riding on the decisions that she would be making in the coming weeks. She didn't want anyone to be hurt because of what she chose, physically or emotionally.

The weather was nice tonight. A slight hint of fall in the air. Seasons in the south were odd. It was pretty much a long summer, two weeks of fall, a colder winter than she would prefer, and two weeks of spring. She would take it though. The air was crisp, the breeze was cool, and the smell of the woods was comforting.

TWENTY-FOUR

Almost everyone was asleep when Brynn made it back home. Everyone except for Max. He was waiting for her in her room.

"How did things go with Quyen tonight babe?" He was stretched out on her bed, wearing pajama pants and nothing else.

She was wondering how much he might

have sensed or seen about what happened. He hadn't had any more of her blood since the battle, so he wasn't in her head as much now. She missed it somewhat, but it was also a relief. He was back down to just sensing emotions for the most part.

"It went pretty well. She didn't tell me everything in the prophecy. We are going to go over it in segments. I was unhappy about that at first, but now I'm grateful that it needs to be that way. It would be total information overload otherwise.

I'll be honest though. Tonight is the first time that I have felt like I really am the girl in the prophecy. Not because of anything she said, but something that I felt deep within me. It's not really something that I can put into words, but I felt it.

"Good. It's about time you started to realize how awesome you are. Can you tell me anything about what she told you? I'm eager to know what your mystica ancestors knew about you before you were even born. It's kinda cool."

"Yeah, I think once it's out there for me to

know about I can tell others if I want to. She told me a few things I already know, like I need to start a new court and bring all mystica together. There were a few things that I didn't know too."

"I can feel you getting nervous. I don't want you to feel like you can't talk to me. Yes, I have been moody lately, but I am working on that. I know it sucks. So, don't be hesitant to tell me about any of it."

She hoped he was right, because this one was a doozy.

"Well, the prophecy does say I am supposed to be the one to lead the court and our people into a new era. It tells of a partner I am supposed to appoint. I represent the fairies and he will represent everyone else."

Max sighed. "It's Gideon, isn't it? That's why you're nervous."

"Yes, it is Gideon."

"When you say partner..."

"I just mean partner. Like, professionally. Trust me, I even asked Quyen to make sure I didn't have a bigger problem on my hands. I stressed about this the whole way home. Please don't take anything out of context."

"I'm not. I have been talking to Vincent about it and he has been helping me work through it. I had already come to terms with the fact that he was going to be sticking around to some extent. It's ok. Am I jealous of him? You bet. I will get over it, though. I don't want to do or say anything to stand in your way."

"Why are you jealous of him?"

"Really? Look at him. He's built like a brick house, he is a great fighter, and he can walk in the sunlight whenever he wants to."

"Come on Max! Have you looked at yourself? You have abs that girls drool over. You are a vampire, so you are naturally an amazing fighter, not to mention the fact that you are super-fast. Besides, you can walk in the sunlight too. You just need a little help beforehand. Give yourself some credit. Plus, I have wanted you since your first day at school. Being with you is a dream come true."

Max grinned and it put Brynn at ease.

"I need to get some sleep babe. We are supposed to be moving back to the compound in the morning. Will you stay with me tonight?"

"What, like in your room with you? I'm pretty sure your dad will kill me the second he realizes I'm in here with you."

"It will be ok. We will just leave the door open. You can even lay on top of the covers if it makes you feel better. I've had one hell of a day and I'd just like to not be alone tonight. I need snuggles."

"If you dad tries to kill me in the morning, it's on you babe." Max hesitantly agreed. It was hard to say no to her.

Hopefully, Vincent wouldn't lose his mind too much when the sun came up. He took his shoes off and laid down next to her. He loved snuggling up to her. For him, there wasn't much better.

They were both a little surprised in the morning when no one came barging in the room yelling about the fast that they were both in there. In fact, when they made it to the kitchen no one even mentioned it.

Everyone was on edge about going back to the compound. Shyan and Madeleine had put in a lot of work over the last week getting things ready and ensuring that there would be no surprises or problems when they showed up with two vampires and a warlock. This really needed to work.

There was one huge benefit to moving with a warlock. Bruce was about to open a portal to the compound, which made the typical tasks associated with moving no longer an issue. No renting a truck, carrying boxes through the yard, or doing back breaking work all day. They would be moved in no time.

Everyone at the compound was shocked to see Brynn when she arrived. She looked much different than she did the last time she was in her home. No one really approached her about it, but based on the stares and whispers, she knew that people were intrigued.

After she put her things in her room, which was exactly how she left it, she began thinking about how to assemble her new court. Where should she start?

She told Quyen that she would call Gideon about his role in the prophecy today. That would probably be a good jumping off point. She closed her bedroom door and dialed his number. He answered after two rings.

"Hey. How's my favorite fairy today?"

"Not bad. Just busy. We all moved back to the compound today."

"Did you miss it?"

"Yes and no. It's a little weird being back here. Everyone keeps staring at me."

"I don't blame them. You're nice to look at. Quyen told me to expect a call from you today."

"Yes sir. I told her I would call you since she was going to talk to you about the prophecy last night."

"So that's why you didn't want me to walk you home, huh?"

"You needed to talk to Quyen. I didn't want to be the one to spill the beans. Plus, she could explain all of it much better than I could. I'm still confused."

"And you were trying to figure out how to tell Max..."

"Yes, that too. It's an awkward situation. While I don't appreciate his jealousy, I still need to consider his feelings. I get why he feels the way he does. So, are you in?"

"Are you sure this is what you want? I know what the prophecy says, but I don't want my presence or involvement to disrupt your life. Is this really going to work?"

"I appreciate that Gideon. Yes, this is what I want. I spoke to Max. He knows that I need you here for this. He agreed to dial it back a bit."

"Ok then, I'm in. What do you need from me?"

"I'm calling a meeting. Can you be at the compound tomorrow at noon?"

"See you then, boss." She could hear his smile as he hung up the phone.

She spent the next few hours speaking

with the elders at the compound, getting their ideas and searching for a few trustworthy fae to be part of the court. That was a more daunting task than she had anticipated.

Thank God she had Madeleine to guide her through this. She got to see firsthand who would be loyal to the former court members when she was being banished.

TWENTY-FIVE

Brynn's nerves were in overdrive as the meeting was approaching. Would everyone take her seriously? She hoped so.

She waited outside for Gideon to arrive at the compound. Things seemed pretty settled with the fairies as far as friendships with other mystica go, but she still didn't fully trust them yet even if they said they were on her side. She didn't want anyone to be rude to Gideon. They needed him to be part of this. Not just because of the prophecy, either. Something in her heart told her that it was important.

He pulled up to the house in what looked like a brand new lifted truck. The vibrant blue paintjob stood out against the black accents. It was a bit surprising. She had him pegged as a motorcycle guy.

"Nice truck." She said as he hopped out and shut the door. He was dressed nicely. His long hair was pulled back. Normally she would make a joke about that kind of hairstyle on men, but he pulled it off.

"Thanks. I have been wanting a new truck for years and I finally bought one last week. I figured after surviving a battle I deserved one." He winked at her as he made his way around to her.

She led him inside the house and through the entryway. They stopped when they made it to the foyer, and she motioned to a chair.

"I hope you don't mind waiting here for a few minutes. I am going to gather everyone else and then we can head to the parlor for the meeting."

Gideon nodded as she scurried out of the room. It wasn't long after that when Max entered the room. He stood up and extended his arm in an attempt to shake hands with Max. His attempt was met with disdain.

"Don't be mistaken. Brynn wants you here. Not me. I don't give a shit what this prophecy supposedly says. Or what your sister claims it says. She only *thinks* she needs you here. She belongs to me. Don't cross me bear cub."

"It doesn't have to be like this dude. I just want to help. I'm not here to step on any toes and interfere with your relationship."

"I doubt that. Just stay out of my way." Max forcefully bumped into Gideon's shoulder as he walked past him and made his way out of the room.

Gideon sat back down as he waited for Brynn. He shook his head as he thought about the ridiculousness of the situation. Was he doing the right thing here or was he just causing more drama? Damn prophecy. Why did it have to include him? He was fine living his simple life before all of this started.

Brynn couldn't believe her eyes. She was about to walk into the room but stayed in the doorway as she heard the conversation between Max and Gideon. She wanted to run after Max and tell him how much of an asshole he was, but she couldn't do that right now. She had a job to do.

"Let's get to the parlor." She said as she finally walked into the room. "They are waiting for us."

When Brynn walked into the room, everyone gave her their full attention.

"As you all know, the courts have betrayed us. They have been holding prisoners and committing horrible atrocities in the other realm. The creatures we conjure have been hunted. Mystica have been in cages for years.

I know it sounds far-fetched and if I hadn't seen it with my own eyes, I might not fully believe it. At the end of our battle, when the remaining court members fled, the glamour that was cast dissolved and they were all there. Suffering.

If we hadn't won the battle, so many more Other mystica factions. If it weren't for all of them, shape shifters, vampires, werewolves, warlocks, we wouldn't be having this conversation today. We have been taught to fear them. This fear is misplaced.

Are you all aware that fairies are the only mystica that do not socialize with others? We keep to ourselves. We shun other fairies when they do not conform and have relationships with them. That needs to end today. They are good people, and we need them if we want to survive.

I have a vision for our new era. We need to have truthful teaching. Our fae children need to know the truth, not what we want them to believe. Because we have been misled for so long, we all need a bit of reeducation.

I also want to have an open forum. Yes, we will have a new court. However, I want anyone who has an idea to feel comfortable presenting it to us. This is how we will grow and continue to improve.

Lastly, we need to help each other. If there is a vampire in need, we should be there. If a shifter wants to lend us a hand, we should accept it. Without these relationships, we are going to be left behind in society.

Now to appoint our new members. If there are no objections, I will lead out new court. If anyone disagrees, please feel free to please speak up."

Brynn paused, giving the others a chance to speak. She was so focused on the task at hand that the thought of someone objecting didn't even cross her mind. She wasn't alone in that, because no one said a word.

"I'm sure everyone has noticed the shifter sitting to my left. His name is Gideon. His bravery during the battle should be applauded. He will be my partner. Think of him as a representative of the other mystica. That being said, you may still seek his counsel in my absence. Vincent, Madeleine, Artemis, Charlois, David, and Dominiq you will lead the new court. We are done with the Seelie name. From now on, it will be known as the High Court.

There is no more good versus evil. There is no room for evil in this new era. Yes, we might all be mischievous by nature. Remember… our people once roamed the heavens, not hades. Let us adjourn for now. We will meet again in three days to discuss ideas and further plans.

After everyone cleared the room, Brynn walked Gideon outside to his truck.

"Thank you for being here today. Maybe we could get together in the next couple of days to discuss our ideas."

"Sounds great. I'm sure after I go home and reflect on the meeting, I will have a few things to talk about. Catch ya later little fairy."

She watched as he drove away and began to dread what was to follow. She walked back inside and made a beeline to her room, keeping her head down and avoiding everybody. Should she let this nonsense go? It would be easier to just act like nothing happened. Would she be able to do that? Probably not. She had to face it. She took a deep breath and sent Max a text asking him to come to her room.

"What's up babe" He asked as he walked

in. "How was your meeting?"

She was already fuming. Anything that she planned to say to him just flew out the window. It was all rage.

"How much of what you say to me is actual bullshit, Max? Do you just tell me what I want to hear?"

"What are you talking about? Did your bear friend talk shit about me?"

She definitely caught him off guard. He already knew what she had to be talking about. He just wasn't sure how she knew. It had to be Gideon.

"He didn't say anything about you, Max. I was standing in the doorway while you were busy being king of the douchebags. Do you realize how stupid you made me look? I had to convince Gideon that it would be okay to be part of this. He didn't want it to cause any problems with us. You told me you understood."

"Come on, Brynn. I just wanted him to know that you are off limits."

"Do you realize that this isn't some high school bullshit we are doing here? This court, this work... it is to make sure that we can all manage to stay alive. What is wrong with you?"

"I don't trust him, Brynn. And at this point, I think you need to make a choice. Him or me."

"I have already chosen you. I am YOUR girlfriend, but I will not remove him from the court. We need him. He is here to stay."

"Okay, then I am out." He stood up and kissed her on the top of the head before walking toward the door.

"What do you mean you're out?"

"I mean I am done dealing with this, I'm done worrying about some meat head shifter. I'm done being your boyfriend."

With his vampire speed, he was gone. She didn't even have time to respond to him. What the hell just happened? How could someone who supposedly cared so much instantly turn so cold?

She didn't need this right now. It was too much. She had so much rebuilding to do. She didn't need Max's drama clouding her judgement.

She sat down on her bed with a notebook and an ink pen. This might not be the best time to brainstorm ideas, but she had to do something. She started with an outline. Old court procedures that needed to be undone, how to build bridges and mend relationships with other mystica, and what direction the new court needed to move toward.

It didn't take long for the day's stress to catch up with her and her eyelids got heavy. She sprawled across her bed and closed her eyes. A short nap never hurt anybody.

TWENTY-SIX

"Hello? Miss Brynn?"

The voice at the door and the accompanying knock startled her awake. She rubbed her eyes as she stood up and made her way to the door. How long had she been asleep? She was surprised to see a female elder standing at her door.

"Hi Stellah. What's up?" Brynn greeted her visitor.

"I am sorry to bother you, but I had an idea that might help you. You see, I know of an old fairy that lives in the woods on the outskirts of town. She keeps to herself, but she sees much. She might be able to advise you on where the former court members have gone."

"I appreciate the offer. It would be nice to have all of the information that is possible. Is she someone that we can trust?"

"Oh yes, we can trust her. I have known her since I was a small fairy. She is very wise. Would you like for me to reach out to her and set up a meeting for you?"

"I would like that. Yes. Please let me know what she says." Brynn paused for a moment. "Would it be dangerous for me to bring a shifter with me?"

"No danger, my dear. Because of her neutrality, she remains a friend to all mystica. I will let you know what I am able to arrange for you."

The elder turned and walked down the hallway. Her short, stubby stature was odd for a fairy. Traditionally, they are pretty thin people. Even the elder fae. Their lifestyle was much different than that of a human. Fairies were healthier people with a naturally high metabolism.

Brynn was nervous. She really did need information, but how would she be able to know who she can actually trust right now? This could either be a great opportunity or a giant set up. She would need to bring Gideon with her. This wasn't a mission she needed to embark on alone.

As she sat on her bed pondering how she would approach all of this, her phone dinged. She jumped at the sound. It was an unfamiliar number. She flipped her phone open to investigate.

It was Stellah. How had she gotten her number?

"She says anytime today is fine. I will text you her address. Let me know if you have any questions before you go."

Today? That was a lot faster than she was

expecting. She hated surprises. If she couldn't make a plan beforehand, it made her nervous. She definitely needed to call Gideon.

"That was fast. I feel like I just left your house. What's up?" He said as he answered his phone.

"I know… surprise! I got a tip on where we can get some information about the missing court members. Do you wanna go with me? I probably shouldn't go alone and since you are my partner in crime now, you were automatically volunteered."

"I'd love to go with you, but will Max be good with that? I'm tired of causing trouble for you, Brynn."

"No, it's cool. We broke up after the meeting today actually. I don't care what he thinks at this point. The fairy said any time today would work for her, but I would like to get there before we are out of sunlight for the day."

"Well, I will be there in twenty minutes then. Just hang tight."

She hung up and gathered her things. She

shoved a notebook into her bag. It was up in the air whether or not she would need it. This could just be a duck mission with nothing to gain in the end. It would be good to be prepared anyway. Maybe she should bring a knife too. She grabbed a small blade out of her drawer and put it in her bag as well.

Gideon could protect her, but there was no reason to leave herself defenseless. She threw her hair up in a ponytail braid and headed outside to wait for her ride.

As soon as she made it out the door, she could see Gideon's truck coming up the driveway. So much for twenty minutes. As he pulled up to the front, he hopped out and ran around the truck to open the passenger door for Brynn.

"Such a gentleman." She chuckled as she got into the truck.

"What can I say. I was raised right." He shut her door and made his way back around.

"I have the fairy's address on my phone. Hopefully, you know where this is because I don't have a clue." She handed her phone to Gideon so he could take a look.

"Yeah, I'm familiar with this area. It's at the end of town. There is a small creek that flows through the woods separating us from the next county. This address is over that way."

"Well, I'm glad one of us knows our way around." She grinned as Gideon put the truck into drive.

"Brynn, I'm sorry about Max."

"I don't really want to talk about it. I just want to move on with my life. There is too much at stake to waste my time dwelling on a guy that doesn't support me."

"Is it going to be okay for me to show up with you at this fairy house?" Gideon asked, making Brynn feel relieved that he was changing the subject.

"Yes, I asked Stellah. I knew that I wanted you to come with me, so I made sure ahead of time. The last thing I want today is more drama."

"Good to know. Thanks for checking beforehand."

"This might all be pretty new to me, but don't worry. I'm not a weak little fairy girl. I got this."

"I believe that." Gideon said with a chuckle. "I saw you in that battle. I may have been busy, but I saw you kicking ass like you had done it a hundred times before."

"Why do you smell like cinnamon?" she blurted out. Instant regret hit her. Why did she say that?

"What?" he laughed heartily. "Where did that come from? You think I smell like cinnamon?"

"Come on. Even if you can't smell it, surely someone has said something about it before."

"Nope. Wait, do I always smell like cinnamon?"

"Yep. Every single time I have been around you, I've smelled it."

"How about this, I'll call and ask Raef."

Gideon dialed the phone and played the

call through his truck speakers.

"Hello?"

"Hey man. I have you on speaker phone. Brynn is here with me. What do I smell like?"

"Hey Brynn. Why the hell are you asking me this dude?"

"Just answer."

"Alright. Like the woods, I guess. You know, like trees and fresh dirt."

"Thank you. Brynn said I smell like cinnamon. I think she's crazy."

Brynn laughed and smacked him on the arm.

"Seriously Raef? You don't smell it?" Brynn interjected.

"Yeah, I'm serious. I love snickerdoodles. I think I would notice. I do know what it means, but that's a story for a different day."

"No way. I wanna know now."

"Tell you what. Call me tomorrow and I'll

tell you. Bye y'all." Raef hung up and Gideon laughed.

"Do you know what story your brother is talking about?"

"No cue princess. I guess we will find out tomorrow."

Brynn huffed and looked out the window. They were driving well off the beaten path. It was a good thing that Gideon drove a truck. This was a pretty rough ride so far. She leaned her head up against the window and closed her eyes.

TWENTY-SEVEN

"Wake up Buttercup."

Brynn sat up straight. She hadn't intended to fall asleep. How many naps was she going to take today?

"How close are we?"

"About five minutes away. I knew you

would want to be awake before we got there.”

“Thank you. I didn’t mean to fall asleep on you. I already took a nap after the meeting today. I didn’t mean to fall asleep then either.”

“No worries. It’s not a bad idea to be rested before this.”

Brynn nodded, taking in her surroundings. They were driving down a very narrow path in the woods. It seemed so desolate out here, she wasn’t convinced that they were on the right track. She trusted Gideon, though.

The truck began to slow down, and she could see dim lights ahead in the distance. As the got closer she began to make out the shape of a house. It was a small cottage style home similar to the one Gideon lived in. There were string lights strung along the edge of the roof. A massive herb garden rested on either side of the front porch.

As Gideon parked the truck, he circled around so the truck was facing away from the house. Good idea. If they had to make a quick getaway there would be one less obstacle.

Gideon hopped out of the truck and made his way to Brynn's door, opening it to let her out. She might joke about it, but she really did enjoy his chivalry. As they made their way to the front door, her heart began to race. She began to doubt her decision to come here. What if she was just putting herself and Gideon in danger?

Gideon knocked on the door three times and took a step back from the door. Brynn was fidgeting, but he seemed calm as a cucumber. She exhaled deeply as the front door opened.

"You must be Brynn." The old fairy bowed to her. "Stellah told me you would be coming. And your shifter friend's name is..." she turned to look at Gideon. She gave him a once over, looking at him from his feet to his head.

"This is Gideon. He is my partner on the new court. I represent the fairies, and he represents all other mystica."

"Well welcome to my home. Both of you. My name is Gwen. Please come in and follow me to the living area."

Gideon positioned himself behind Brynn

and closed the door behind them. He scanned their surroundings as they made her way through the house, looking for any other people that might be in the house.

As they made it to the living room, Gwen motioned for them to take a seat on the couch.

"If you two will give me just a moment, I will go get us some tea."

"That's not necessary. You don't need to wait on us." Brynn said. She was already a bit embarrassed that the old woman had bowed to her. She didn't need to be served. Even if she was thirsty."

"Nonsense. Any guest in my home gets tea. Now, wait here and I will be back in a moment." Gwen quickly disappeared. She walked with a bit of a hunch. Her face was covered in deep wrinkles. She had many necklaces with crystals around her neck.

Brynn and Gideon sat there silently looking around the room. There were many herbs and differently sized and shaped crystals all over. The home was clean, but cluttered. Multiple journals stacked on the table. An old open faced medicine cabinet full of tinctures.

"Alright my dearies, here you go." Gwen said as she reentered the room. She handed each of them a cup of tea.

"Different teas?" Brynn asked, noticing that her tea was a different color than Gideon's.

"Ah yes. Different mystica, different needs. It would be a travesty to serve everyone generically made tea. Now, let's sit and discuss the reason that you came here today. You want to know what I know."

Brynn mustered up the strength to take a sip of her tea. Gross. It was bitter and strong. She felt like she had grass in her mouth. It had quite a tang, which she assumed was from too many herbs. Herbal selections were never her favorite. Gideon downed his in only a few sips, sighing with a sense of enjoyment. His must have been a lot better.

"Do you live here alone?"

"Yes Miss Brynn. I prefer to keep a small circle. The woods offer wonderful solitude. It is peaceful out here."

"Are you not afraid to be out here alone? What if something happens? What would you do?"

"Well, I get around pretty well for an old gal. If the day comes when that is no longer true, I will probably move on from here."

"How much do you know about what is going on right now?"

"Quite a bit. I know of the battle you had with the court in the other realm. I also know what was going on in the other realm before you got there."

"If you knew, why didn't you try to do something about it? Didn't you want it to stop?"

"While I may not have agreed with what was going on, it was not my business. I am too old to do anything, even if I wanted to. It's just what it is."

Brynn didn't like her answer. She wanted to say more, but now wasn't the time to be disrespectful.

"What have you heard about the remaining court members?"

"From what I heard; they have all left town. There will make it pretty difficult to find them. I wouldn't expect to hear anything from them for quite a while. They will need time to regroup. However, I will warn you. They will start to reach out to fairies that were loyal to them in the past. They will try to recruit them and some of them will go no matter what you do. Loyalty is difficult to sway."

Brynn made a mental note to stay extra guarded when talking to anyone that wasn't in the battle with her.

"Do you have any idea what they will try once they feel like their group is strong enough?"

"That I do not know. We fairies are mischievous dear. Who knows what we are all capable of."

Brynn nodded and put her hand on Gideon's knee.

"I really appreciate our willingness to speak with us today. I'm afraid we must be going. If you hear anything, please don't hesitate to reach out to me."

Gwen nodded as she and Gideon stood up. She remained in her seat as they showed themselves out.

"What do you think?" Gideon asked as they began to drive away.

"Well, it wasn't a total waste of time. It wasn't super informative either. At least it sounds like we have a little time to get organized before we have anything to worry about."

"I suppose you are right. Not a total loss, though. That tea was delicious."

"Are you crazy?" Brynn laughed out loud. "That was the worst tea I have ever had. It tasted like a cup of watery grass with herbs. And it gave me a stomachache!"

"Well, mine tasted like vanilla and cinnamon. It was great. I wonder why she gave us different drinks."

"Who knows. She's old. It probably made sense to her. I just wish mine could have tasted as wonderful as yours apparently did."

Gideon shrugged his shoulders as he tried to navigate the narrow path he was driving down. It had gotten dark, and the woods were much harder to see through now. The last thing he wanted was to wreck his truck out in the middle of nowhere.

Brynn turned on the radio and closed her eyes, losing herself in thought for the remainder of the drive home. There were so many scenarios running through her head. Her brain was getting crowded.

As Gideon pulled into her driveway, she stretched her arms and yawned. He parked and she just sat and waited for him to open her door. Once the door was closed behind her, he gave her a hug. The embrace lingered for longer than she expected.

"Thank you for coming with me today, Gid." She said as he released his grip on her.

"Thank you for inviting me. It might not have been everything that you hoped it would be, but I'm glad I got to be there with you for it. You're not bad company either. I could get used to it." He gave Brynn a wink.

"Me too." Brynn said as she yawned again.

"Get inside and get your third nap of the day in." Gideon chuckled.

"Ok. Good night." She stuck her tongue out at him.

He blushed. She couldn't help but smile. She had never seen him blush before.

"See you soon. I hope."

"I'll call you tomorrow." She waved as she headed inside.

TWENTY-EIGHT

Brynn smiled as she walked inside the house.

"Where have you been all day? We've been worried about you." Vincent was hovering by the door.

She didn't even think to tell anyone else she was leaving. Thinking back on it, that probably would have been a good idea. Did they know about Max?

"Stellah said that she knew an old fairy that might have information that would help us. I went to see her."

"Why didn't you say anything to anyone? That could've been dangerous."

"I don't know. It all happened so fast. I didn't even think of it. Gideon went with me. I was safe."

"I appreciate that he was there to help you, but you being outnumbered isn't the only thing to worry about. What if it was a setup? What if it was false information?"

"You're right. I should have said something. It would have been smart to see if anyone knew this fairy or not. Sorry dad."

"I'm not criticizing you, Brynn. You're not in trouble. Until you are more seasoned though, you really need to communicate with us for things such as this.

I know you have had a bad day, so I'll cut you some slack. I heard about you and Max. There's got to be a lot on your mind right now."

"How did you find out?"

"Max told me. He asked if he could go live at my house for a while. I asked him why he wanted to, and he told me that the two of you broke up."

"Did he tell you why?"

"He didn't tell me much. I'm not dumb, though. I have been watching him and trying to help guide him. There is a lot of jealousy in him. He feels threatened by Gideon. I told him before that he needed to reel it in. I'm guessing that he didn't."

"That's pretty much sums it up. I feel bad, though. He is in this crazy life now because of me. I feel guilty letting him experience it without me... alone."

"Honey, you cannot feel that sense of responsibility for him forever. Everyone makes their own choices. He made his. You made yours. You will both figure it out. I will keep up with the sunlight spell for him. He will be ok."

Brynn nodded. What an exhausting day this had been.

"Did you get any information from the fairy you went to see?"

"Nothing that I didn't already assume. It was confirmation at least. It sounds like we have a little time to get things organized before we have to worry about the former court."

"That's good to hear. I figured it would be so."

"There she is." Madeleine said as she entered the room. "We have been worried about you girl."

"Sorry Aunt Madeleine. I didn't mean to worry you guys. I should have stopped to think about it before I left."

"It seems Brynn went on an adventure today to see a fairy on the edge of town." Vincent quickly brought her up to speed.

"What was this fairy's name?"

"Uhhhh. I think it was Wren. I'm bad with names. I can ask Gideon. I'm sure he will remember."

"Please do the next time you speak with him. I know a few and I just want to make sure you are safe. There are dangerous fairies on the outskirts. They live a secluded life for a reason. You can't trust a rogue. Bring me with you next time. I'm always up for a trip."

"You look exhausted my daughter. Go get some rest. We can talk about it in the morning."

He was right. She was exhausted. She may have had two naps already, but she needed another. Gideon was right.

She made her way to the bedroom and had to fight the urge to crawl into bed. She wanted to shower first. After gathering a change of clothes, she made her way into her ensuite bathroom. She turned the shower to a temperature that could probably boil a lobster and got in.

This had been such an emotional day. She just wanted to wash Max, this day, and the woods off of her. You can't wake up and have a good morning with yesterday's bad vibes all over you. She gave her scalp a massage as she rubbed shampoo through her hair. This was exactly what she needed. She rinsed her hair, finished up her hair care routine, and got out.

She was too tired to do much more of a night routine, so she cast a quick drying spell, got dressed, and finally crawled into bed. She made a quick mental note to figure out the spell for shaving your legs. That would come in handy. Why hadn't she thought about it before?

There were so many things running through her mind. It was overwhelming. She was beginning to doubt her decision to meet with this fairy. This could have backfired in a big way. Was she trustworthy? How would she even be able to find that out?

She focused hard to block everything out. No more boys, no more fighting, no more drama. As soon as her shields were up, she fell right asleep.

TWENTY-NINE

Brynn woke up suddenly, drenched in sweat and feeling disoriented and confused. She hadn't expected to fall asleep as quickly as she did. She looked at the clock and was surprised to see that it was after midnight. While she did feel rested, as soon as she woke up the earlier events came flooding back in.

She changed out of her sweaty pajamas,

slipping on a flowy white dress and sandals. Normally she wouldn't go for a walk this late, but it felt like exactly when she needed.

When she got outside, she glanced up at the sky. It was such a clear, crisp night. There were so many stars in the sky. It was hard to believe her eyes. The full moon was so big that it almost looked fake. She could feel the pull of it. Magic was much more potent during a full moon. Who knew what kind of spells she could pull off on a night like this.

Was this feeling normal? This pull she was feeling.

She began walking with no destination in mind. Her heart was guiding her. Instead of taking her normal route to the park, she headed toward the woods. Hopefully, she wouldn't end up regretting this. She didn't exactly change into woods exploring attire.

The sound of the woods was so enchanting. The owls were cooing their nighttime songs. Steady humming from the crickets and cicadas set a background tune that almost seemed intentional. Leaves and twigs quietly cracked under her feet as she made her way through. There were no trails this deep, but she had an easy time making it through.

She looked around when she made it to a clearing. It was like a secret or forgotten meadow. As she peered to the other side of the clearing, she was startled to see someone standing there. She rubbed her eyes to make sure it was real.

"Brynn? Is that you?"

"Gideon? What are you doing out here?"

"I'm not really sure. I was asleep and woke up suddenly. It's hard to explain, but I just felt compelled to go for a walk. This is where I ended up. Why are you out here? Do you normally walk in these woods?"

"No. I've never been out here before. I got here the same as you. I had a bad day today. After finally shutting myself down for the night, I went for a walk to clear my head. Now I'm here with you."

They had been moving closer to each other throughout the conversation. Now they were within arm's reach.

"I'm sorry that today was a bad day for you. Did something else happen? You seemed okay when I dropped you off last night."

She sighed, dropping to the ground. The grass was soft. Gideon sat down beside her.

"I heard what Max said to you. After you left, I confronted him about it. We argued and ended up breaking up. He left the compound. Apparently, he is living at my dad's house for right now."

"I'm sorry. I wasn't going to tell you about what Max said before the meeting. I feel like this is my fault. Now you are hurting because of me. I should have just stayed out of the court stuff."

"That's the thing... I'm not upset. I feel relieved. You aren't supposed to feel like that after a breakup. It makes me feel like an asshole."

"You're not an asshole, Brynn. You're perfect."

Gideon grabbed her face and kissed her. The tingles she felt when they kissed before were there again, but they were more intense this time. In fact, she could have sworn that she saw sparks when his lips touched hers.

"I'm not apologizing this time." He said before kissing her again.

He moved his hand through her hair, holding the side of her head. She wrapped her arms around him, enjoying the strength and heat of his body. He slowly guided her backward until she was laying down in the grass on her back.

"I have wanted you since I first laid eyes on you." He said as his kisses started to travel further down.

Their kissing didn't stop as he moved until he was halfway on his side and half on top of her.

"Do you want me to stop?" he asked softly.

"No." she said simply. Her whole body trembled as the tingles intensified.

As she rubbed her fingers across his skin, she could feel the beast stirring within him. Could he hurt her? She had seen him in battle. She knew what he was capable of.

He slid the straps of her dress off of her shoulders and slowly pulled the whole thing down until it was off. She shivered as he began kissing her neck and collarbone.

"Are you cold?"

"No... tingly."

"Me too. Way more than last time."

"Me too. Maye it's the moon."

"Maybe it's destiny." He smiled at her.

She pulled him back to her while pushing the waistband of his shorts down. He grinned, hesitating for a moment.

"I'm not wearing any underwear. I was in bed before I came here."

"Good." She smiled before pushing them all the way off.

The veracity when they became one made her gasp. She was completely overcome with emotion. It was powerful. Not only did she feel ignited in her soul, but she also felt...

complete.

"Tell me you're mine." he said, staring into her eyes.

She giggled, not expecting his request.

"Tell me, Brynn. Say you are mine." He pulled her hair, making her back arch a bit. Why did she like this so much?

God he was strong. She felt so small beneath him. So vulnerable.

"I'm yours, Gideon." She breathed in his ear.

He moaned loudly as the ground shook beneath them.

With each stride, she got a little more lost in the moment. Even if she had fantasized about this, she couldn't have imagined it would be this good. She was lost in complete ecstasy.

He sighed with pleasure before rolling down beside Brynn. She was still trying to catch her breath. They laid in the soft grass, smiling and enjoying just being there together.

"Did you feel that too?" Gideon asked quietly, almost as if he were afraid to say it out loud.

"I don't know what to call it... It was something powerful, whatever it was."

He kissed the top of her head before getting put. He stuck his hand out for hers, pulling her up to face him.

"Your hair..." Gideon said with a look of surprise. "The blue is gone."

She looked down to see shiny brown hair. There was no more blue, but it had been replaced with extra shimmer. She just chuckled and shrugged her shoulders.

"I don't want this to be a onetime thing, Brynn. I know you have a lot going on in your life right now. I just want to be part of it."

"I want that too."

She smiled as he handed her dress to her. They put their clothes back on and stood there for a moment, both trying to decide what to do next.

A crack of thunder sounded, making both of them jump. Before either of them could say a word, there was a bright flash of light and they were suddenly surrounded by stars. They weren't just above them in the sky anymore. They were all around them. So, close they were within arm's reach. A loud, almost ethereal voice came from above.

"The stars are in place and the future of the fae and their friends is in your hands, Brynn and Gideon. Together you can save our race. Brynn, you must guide Gideon through life. Never lead him astray and never turn your back on him. Gideon, you must protect Brynn at all costs. Love her, cherish her, and help her let her light shine. It is time for you both to fulfill your destiny."

At the last word, there was a bright flash as the stars rescinded back to the sky and everything settled back into place.

"Your collarbone... there is a small tattoo now. That wasn't there before, was it?" Gideon softly traced it with his finger.

"You have one too now. It looks like a constellation."

"So does yours. Which constellation?" he asked as he tried to look at the new mark on his chest. It was too high up. He couldn't get a look at it. He was going to have to rely on Brynn to describe it to him.

"I'm not sure. I don't think I have seen it before. What about mine?"

"I think I have seen it before, but I can't quite put my finger on it. What shape is mine?"

"It's kinda like... well, it kinda looks like a fairy."

At this point, Gideon couldn't help but laugh.

"What's so funny?"

"Yours looks like a bear. That's what's funny. The stars always seem to have a sense of humor."

"Normally I roll my eyes when I see people with couple's tattoos. I think we can pull this off, though." She laughed as she traced his tattoo with her finger. A little representation of her.

Gideon put Brynn's face in his hand.

"What the stars said...I promise, Brynn." He smiled as he gazed into her eyes.

"Me too, Gideon. I promise.

PROPHECY OF A FAE

BOOKS ONE AND TWO
NOW
AVAILABLE

ROGUE FAE
BOOK THREE
COMING
SOON

READ AHEAD FOR A SNEAK PEEK OF BOOK TWO

SPELLBOUND
PROLOGUE

"Have you seen her?" Fiona asked with a panicked tone in her voice.

"No. I've looked everywhere. She isn't answering her phone either."

"It's not like her to disappear like this. She was acting weird last night when she went to bed."

"What do you mean she was acting weird? What was she doing?"

"Didn't she call you? She calls you every night if you're not staying here."

"No, I never heard from her. I assumed she fell asleep. She was really tired yesterday." Gideon ran his fingers through his hair, frustrated.

"She just seemed a bit on edge. You know, pacing a lot, acting worried. Asked her what was wrong, but she just waved her hand as if to say nothing. After I told her goodnight, she went into her room. That's the last that I saw her."

"Shit. Go ask your mom if she has seen her. I'll go talk to Vincent. Call me if you figure anything out."

Damnit, Brynn. Where was she? She hadn't been acting herself the last few days. She was distant and distracted.

Ouch! Not again... The sharp pain in his chest took him straight to his knees. His tattoo had been doing that for days now. It had to be about Brynn. It was her tattoo. He pulled out his phone and dialed Vincent.

"Hey Gideon. What's up?"

"Hey. Have you heard from Brynn today?"

"No, I haven't. Is everything ok?"

"I don't know. No one has seen her. It's unlike her. She always at least tells someone where she is going."

"Hmm. Find Madeleine. If nothing else

Bruce might be able to figure something out. He's got powers far beyond what any of us have."

"Ok, thanks. I'll let you know when I find her."

Gideon hung up the phone and started looking for Madeleine. Hopefully Fiona had already been able to track her down. His tattoo throbbed once again. Not now. He had to keep going.

He started walking toward the living room. It could be difficult to find someone at the compound. There were always so many people in and out. He had been spending a lot of time here lately, but he still wasn't used to it. He could hear the faint sound of voices up ahead, so he picked up the pace.

"Gideon! I was just about to call you. No one had seen her today." Fiona frowned. Shyan and Madeleine were standing with her looking worried.

"Vincent hasn't heard from her either." He shrugged his shoulders, feeling defeated.

"Gideon. The fairy you and Brynn went to visit in the woods. Do you remember her name? Brynn wasn't sure and said that I should ask you." Madeleine had been meaning to ask him this already, but it kept slipping her mind.

"Yeah. That makes sense. Brynn is terrible with names. The fairy we went to see called herself Gwen."

"Shit! Someone go find Bruce." Everyone froze in place. Her sudden panic startled everyone. After a second, Gideon began to run for Bruce's room.

"Hurry!" Madeleine's voice disappeared behind him.